THRILL IN A KILL

Thrill In A Kill
Edited & Compiled by Uma Bokil
Print Edition

First Published in India in 2021
Inkfeathers Publishing, New Delhi 110095

Copyright © Inkfeathers Publishing, 2021
Cover Design © 2021 Inkfeathers Publishing

www.inkfeathers.com

THRILL IN A KILL

Edited & Compiled by

Uma Bokil

Inkfeathers Publishing

CO-AUTHORED BY

Susan Bowman | Prajwal Shukla | Yashika Rawal

Saloni Wagle | Srikanth Palaparthy | Hari Pudipeddi

Akhilesh Mahender | Salbaz Sayeed | Sameem Hassain

Darshini Parthiban| Himanshu Sukhala | Anamika Kundu

Kristin Carmen | Karthik C | Deepshikha Saw

Santhosh Ganesan Manish Nair | Manoj Vaz

Geetika K. Bakshi | Aaron Dsouza | D. H. Holmes

Sudha Ramnath | Uma Bokil

CONTENTS

ABOUT THE EDITOR

Uma Bokil

Lost in the beauty of words, Uma is a young girl in her twenties from Pune. She befriended books at a young age, courtesy of her mother, and fell in love with the mere existence of them a few good reads later. Not being able to fathom how something bundled up into pages could have such an effect on her, she dove deeper.

Growing up, her career choices danced like a butterfly in a garden filled with flowers. From an engineer to a dentist to a surgeon to what-not, she slowly came to terms with her love for writing but was apprehensive about looking at it as a career.

The year 2020 and the lockdown were life-turners for a lot of people, and it was no exception for her. At the age of nineteen and lost in terms of what her actual career path was meant to be, she decided to try her hand at writing and editing. And once she started, there was no turning back.

She co-authored in one or two anthologies before venturing out into one of her own. This is her grind, and she aims to do it full-time, and is excited to learn as much about writing, editing and the world in general as she can. According to her, she has found something that gives her utmost joy and satisfaction. The butterfly has finally found her flower.

PREFACE

There's a whole new world of adventures lurking in between two words and two lines. Such is the beauty of books. I grew up reading about Cinderella's lost shoe to the ultimate heroism of Harry against Voldemort and the sorrowful death of Augustus Waters. But nothing has fascinated me like a good murder mystery.

Reading the works of Sidney Sheldon, Robin Cook and Jeffrey Archer stirred up something inside me that got me hooked to the concept of twists, turns, and jaw-dropping incidents, all in one story, pulling me to its depths and leaving me wanting for more. So, when I had to decide a theme for my debut anthology, the answer called out to me.

I decided to start off my professional writing experience with an anthology because it is primarily one of the best platforms, as it brings together exceptional and thoroughly inspirational writers from various nooks and corners of the world, all packed together into one amazing book filled with wonderful tales.

Thrill in a Kill is not just a collection of your regular murder fiction, but instead, a treasure of short stories that will induce goosebumps all over your body. Stories by talented authors from not just across India but overseas have been compiled together to make this dream come true.

Initially, I had reservations when it came to finding like-minded people who were just as big murder-mystery fanatics as I was but then I came across some of the most brilliant writers I could have the privilege of knowing. To say that I was overjoyed when these authors with a marvellous flair for writing chose to be a part of this venture would be one of the biggest understatements. Every writer brought something wonderful to the table, and I caught myself reading and re-reading these amazing stories, sometimes, not even as an editor!

Each story, as it unravels, leads you to a different level of thrill, no pun intended, and some in a different time or space altogether. While others leave you agape in horror with their open endings, some of them give you a sense of closure, as a means to portray that even within the crime scene, happy endings do exist. With every plot uniquely woven, it's bound to leave you shocked to the bone. May it be a twist that awaits just around the corner, or a hunch on a wrong suspect, or a backstory that will completely throw the reader off. This anthology will swoon you with its rollercoaster of suspense, love, sorrow, tragedy, surprise, and much, much more.

Compiling this anthology has helped me evolve not just as writer, but as a person, too. It has given me numerous lessons along the way, many of which will be etched in my memory as far as my life goes. It has connected me with writers from whom I've had the chance to learn a lot, put consistency and dedication in a completely new light for me, and upgraded me to a level where I have newfound respect for all editors. Needless to say, the quality of content I have received for the anthology has been so welcoming that being a compiler actually ended up becoming a party.

Without further ado, my fellow writers and I invite you to turn over the page and become a part of this precious joyride that will certainly add some extra thrill to your bookshelves, pun fully intended. By the end of this journey, we hope it will become as important to you as it has become to us. Thank you for choosing us. We'll see you on the other side.

1

VICTIM

by Susan Bowman

She sat with her back tightly wedged into the corner; knees bent and drawn up under her chin like a little girl. Although she was seventeen, she could easily pass for twelve. Snivelling and snotty, her hair was knotted and fine, like a baby's, as it fell forward to form a veil across her face. She gently rocked to-and-fro, licking her dry lips after nibbling her fingernails.

Small as a mouse, she was dressed in a hospital-type gown which the desk sergeant had given her when he had checked her in and had taken her own clothes away for forensics. The gown was dirty-white and much too big for her little frame. The girl would jump at any sound. Seemingly afraid, and to be honest, it wasn't surprising. She wiped her nose with the back of her hand, and a string of snot joined her body.

"Don't you want your tea, lovely? You should 'ave a bit of toast," smiled the canteen lady, but the girl didn't even glance at her. The lady wobbled along the corridor with her trolley, cups and saucers rattling like an out-of-tune orchestra. Then, the lady stopped to speak to Geraldine as her chins jiggled in the process, while she wiped her hands on a grubby apron. "That little thing in there," she said, pointing behind her with a fat thumb, "she is such a tiny, skinny thing, and she ain't touched 'er toast."

Geraldine thought she'd seen it all in this place. She sighed and turned back to her keyboard and continued typing. "You never know what's going to happen one day to the next," she said, "nothing surprises me anymore."

The girl was Elizabeth, the only child of Ms. Mary Lloyd, a single mother. Ms. Lloyd said that Elizabeth's father had died when she was seven. An abusive man, he used to terrorise the family. The mother said without embarrassment that it was a relief when he died in a domestic incident.

"The hopeless drunk tripped over Elizabeth's Barbie car at the top of the stairs, lost his footing, fell and cracked his head on the tiled floor at the bottom. He was a bad man, violent even. He never hurt Elizabeth, but that's not to say he wouldn't have. He put me in the hospital twice," she told the sergeant. Sadly, Ms. Lloyd never found the strength nor the courage to press charges.

Elizabeth attended the local secondary school in West Haddon. She was a good student, reportedly very quiet and without friends. Her tutor voiced concerns more than once about her isolation. One possible explanation for her antisocial behaviour was that she was the main caretaker for her mum, who was partially abled. The social worker involved with the family at the time of her father's death pointed out that this kind of isolation was common amongst young caretakers.

Now, the main concern was to get her examined by the police surgeon. The girl was taken into an interview room for questioning. She was getting fidgety and anxious. Perspiration covered her brow which she wiped with her palm, then rubbed her hands along her thighs. She glanced, first at the man and then at the woman across the narrow table, and then rested her beautiful, cold-grey eyes on the solicitor sitting next to her, who gently assured her that he would look out for her.

The male detective was losing patience by the minute. He got up and paced around the small room, rubbing the back of his neck. "Look," he said, "This is really not helping us, Elizabeth. We will get to the bottom of this, you can be sure of that; the sooner, the better. You must see that?" He questioned, appealing to her understanding. Now, the lady officer with the kind eyes reached across the desk and rested a hand on Elizabeth's shoulder. Even this gentle act made Elizabeth flinch. The officer immediately withdrew her hand and straightened herself. The girl still wouldn't speak.

The officers went out for some tea and left the girl seated, hunched on the hard chair. After a while, the canteen lady entered and said, "Nice cuppa tea, lovely? 'Ow about a sandwich, I've got cheese and 'am. Which would you like, dear?" She prodded.

The girl looked at the fat canteen lady with her cold eyes and said nothing.

***

Across the hall in a separate room, sat the boy. He was eighteen but could pass for mid-twenties with his shaved head and a stubble, which made him look threatening. He was well-built; not big but toned. His bare arms boasted several tattoos which were photographed and logged on the crime sheet. He had already been DNA'd and fingerprinted, and now he was being interviewed. He had given his name as Michael Davies, and his attitude was bad – really bad.

He was the polar opposite of Elizabeth. Sitting tall on the chair, he puffed his chest out and smirked. He intimidated even Detective Jenson, a big man. Jenson asked for a uniform to be present while he questioned this young man.

"So," said Jenson. "You going to tell me what happened last night?"

"Well," said the teenager, "what yer wanna know?"

The detective considered his response. Davies was a smarmy git and was going to be hard work. "How do you know Elizabeth Lloyd?"

"We was at school together, innit? We was signin' on together, too," he laughed and rocked back in his seat. "I didn't really know her. Yer get me?"

This nasty piece of work was not going to be generous with answers. Jenson was losing his cool. This was a man you wouldn't want to see when angry. Making sure that the uniformed police officer was not about to turn his back, Jenson walked out.

***

The girl was being examined by the police surgeon who was worried that she hadn't uttered a single word. Concerned about her mental health, he tried again to establish a dialogue with her.

"You know, I can't help you if you won't talk to me," he said, "I am not here to make judgments. I just want to know if you need any medical attention. Can I do anything for you?" Elizabeth looked at him then shook her head no.

The doctor told the duty sergeant that although physically okay, there were some serious concerns regarding the girl's mental welfare. "She's clearly in shock. I can't tell if she's capable of giving a statement. I think we need to get a psyche over to assess her, just to be on the safer side."

***

It had been 15 hours since a jogger had run past the couple and caught a glimpse of what he assumed to be the body of a young lad lying on the ground. The shaken-up jogger was rushed to the hospital after showing symptoms of a heart attack. Before his collapse, the witness reported seeing the youngster on the ground with two other people. He remembered seeing one kneeling beside the body and the male suspect kicking the prostrate lad.

He described them as white and young; one boy, one girl, both dressed in casual clothing – probably jeans. They were inside a small copse which was frequented by drug users. Emergency services arrived before the pair realized they'd been spotted.

As it turned out, the victim was already dead at the scene and the body was taken directly to Harebridge hospital mortuary to establish the cause of death. However, a preliminary report from the scene stated that the victim had most definitely died from head injuries.

***

Elizabeth Lloyd, on being interviewed by an on-call psychiatrist, was deemed fit for 'due process'. His report would go on to state that '...the young girl showed obvious signs of trauma, but...'

"Bloody hell, all you need is one look at her. She is compos mentis, little thing. What's she here for?"

"C'mon, you know I can't tell you that, but if you reckon she's fit to be interviewed, hopefully, you'll soon find out – that's if she ever opens her mouth."

It was a couple of hours later that Ms. Lloyd brought some clothes for Elizabeth to change into. The girl did not speak to her mother either but was quick to get into jeans and a sweater. Elizabeth was escorted back into the interview room for another attempt.

"Are you ready to speak with us now?" asked Detective Jenson, "You're really not helping yourself by remaining silent." The detective leaned across the table to make eye contact with the girl. The only sound Elizabeth made was the constant sniffling back of tears.

"My client has every right to remain silent as you are fully aware, detective. I really don't see what this harassment is achieving. Have you questioned Mr. Davies, yet? He may be more forthcoming." *Bloody lawyers. Right to remain silent was a bloody nuisance; all it ever achieved was a delay. They all talked in the end, couldn't help themselves,* thought Jenson in disapproval.

The detective conceded defeat, and left the interview room, he instructing a waiting WPC to escort Elizabeth to the sick bay 'where she would be more comfortable'.

***

All Michael Davies wanted was to lie down and sleep. *These pigs need to shut up so I can get some shuteye,* he thought to himself.

"I've told you over and over again what happened. I was going to meet my mate and I more or less tripped over them. I didn't know him, I haven't seen him before, and I just stopped to check him out. The guy was just lying there, man, with his fucking head caved in," Davies rambled, frustrated.

"Where were you going at such a late hour?" Jenson, checking his notes, asked, "At 1:45 a.m. give or take?"

"Meeting a mate, man, okay? I was going to meet a friend. Ain't no law, is there, that I don't know about?"

"Don't get smart, son," snapped Jenson, "you're already in a whole lot of trouble." The detective rose from his seat, arched his back against the screaming pain, and took a few steps so that he was directly behind Davies' chair.

Leaning in close, he said, "We have a witness that saw you putting the boot in while this fella was on the ground, plus we have Miss Lloyd's statement." Jenson was bluffing, of course, but the chap didn't know it. Jenson's words had the desired effect. Feeling rather pleased with himself, he added, "We also have a dead body."

"What the fuck… he's dead? And which witness, and what statement?" Davies stuttered. The penny dropped, and along with it, a realisation.

Jenson smirked. "Worried now, are you, son?" he sneered.

"Listen, I ain't got nothing to be worried about, 'cept smokin' a bit of weed, maybe. That bloke was on the ground when I saw him; she was kneeling next to him and I didn't put no boot in. I tried to roll him over with my foot so I could see him; see if he was breathing," said Davies.

"That's not what we heard, Mr. Davies, not at all," Jenson replied.

"That witness you got must have seen what she was doing, right?" said Davies, panicking now. Beads of sweat trickled down his brow which he swept away impatiently. Clearly, the detective's comments were worrisome. He could go down for this. He needed the cops to believe that it was Elizabeth Lloyd who battered the victim's head with a lump of rock, a rock which she still held in her hand as he had tripped into the clearing.

"This is shit, man, I didn't do nothing. The girl, it was the girl, she done it. She was the one that done it. You've got to believe me, man." Davies, with his elbows on his knees, held his head and bawled like a baby. "I didn't do it, you have to believe me."

Until that moment, detective Jenson had him squarely in the frame for the brutal slaying of the young man now identified as Mark Evans, the 16-year-old victim of a bloody and crazed attack. Surely that little girl could not have done such a thing. Surely she was innocent? Only now, seeing the kid cry so openly and his hard man act having had disintegrated made Jenson have second thoughts.

He had a record for petty theft, a TWOC or two, and a bag of snatch, but not violence. He himself was a victim of sorts: deprived, inner-city childhood, fatherless, running the streets at an early age – Jenson knew all that was no excuse for delinquent behaviour, but he also understood that it went a long way to explain it. And what could the motive have been – drugs, gangs? Jenson didn't believe so; there was no evidence to suppose that this murder bore such a criminal connection. To him, it seemed to bear all the signs of a domestic incident.

Elizabeth was seven when her father died in a domestic incident.

Jenson stretched his back again as the long night took its toll on him. I must get back to that physio, he logged a mental note before returning to the case. Davies had been taken back to his cell with a cup of piss water – what passed for tea in the station. He was really shaken up by the latest interview and Jenson was aware that although the lad had refused a brief, he really ought to be represented now, especially as he would probably be charged.

Still, the way Davies described the scene he had come across did sound plausible. Perhaps it was Jenson's desperation for a lead or plain frustration that got him thinking about having another go at the girl. Whichever it was, he called through to the desk and asked WPC Choudhary to bring the girl back for further questioning.

"She's actually sleeping now, can it wait for a bit, sir?"

"No, Dev. I need to speak with her now; you can sit in and get the duty brief, too."

***

"For the benefit of the tape, those present are DI Jenson, WPC Choudhary, Miss Elizabeth Lloyd, and duty solicitor, Mr. Nigel Jarvis." The DI began the questioning.

"Miss Lloyd, Mr. Davies has given a very incriminating statement, claiming that Mark Evans was already on the ground when he stumbled across you. You were kneeling beside the body and you had in your hand what will, in due course, turn out to be the murder weapon. Miss Lloyd, I need you to consider your answer very carefully before you speak. Did you strike Mr. Evans?"

Elizabeth Lloyd finally looked up and directly into the detective's eyes and replied, "Yes, yes I did." The girl calmly addressed Jenson, "I did. I had to make him stop."

"I'm sorry, 'make him stop'? Can you explain?" Jenson glanced over to the policewoman who was staring at Elizabeth in disbelief, amazed both at the sudden response and at the words. "Elizabeth, you must be certain of what you are saying. You are being recorded. Anything you say will be used as evidence against you. Do you understand?" she said.

"Tell us what happened, Elizabeth," Jenson prodded gently.

Elizabeth took a deep breath and began to speak in a soft, quiet voice. She looked down at her hands. "We were sitting in the woods, looking at the stars. We had a little smoke and were laughing, having a crack – it was fun. And then, he ruined it. He started at me, you know, the way men always do, touching and groping. I kept telling him to stop and he wouldn't. I had to make him leave me alone. I had to make him stop." She sighed. "Just like I had to make daddy stop."

2

THE BRIDGE CASE

by Susan Bowman

Transcript of a statement by Susan Brown. 31st March, 2020

Those present: D. C. Joanne Edwards; D. S. David Smith; Mrs. Susan Brown.

D. S. SMITH: *Please tell us what you remember about the events transpired on 26th March.*

S. BROWN: *Okay, so it's very hard to know where to start.*

D. S. SMITH: *Right from the beginning, please.*

S. BROWN: *Sheila had been acting strange lately; she even got things confused; we even joked about it. But once, she went ballistic just because I put smoked salmon on the sandwiches. On 26th March, a mighty row took place. I've no idea how long Sheila and Vanessa had been fighting, but things sounded really worked up. Vanessa was screaming at Sheila, saying, "You miserable cow! No wonder he's not interested in you. You're about as attractive as..." I couldn't believe my ears. Vanessa and Sheila had been school mates. They did lots of stuff together, went on holidays together. Just as I walked into the room, Sheila yelled, "If you weren't such a tart and had laid it on a plate for him, he wouldn't have looked twice at you. You thought nothing about stealing somebody else's husband just because you couldn't keep yours happy." Sheila had gone too far. Vanessa picked something up from the sideboard and flung it with full force at Sheila. The next thing I remember, we – me, Vanessa, and Barb were standing over a bleeding Sheila. Time stood still, until Barb said, "Jeez – Sue, call for an ambulance, hurry."*

I read the statement for the second time. We sure had a case here. Vanessa Jones had acted with malice. Although she was provoked, she didn't have a strong defence. She had intended to harm the victim.

Having been with the Crown Prosecution Service for eight years, I'd been given this case, and therefore, been invited to witness an interview with Vanessa. There seemed little to-no evidence for murder, rather more of involuntary manslaughter. I half-expected the coroner to report it as an accident.

Vanessa sat in a holding cell, the plain brickwork and cold starkness of the place making the scene look desolate. She sat still, her head hung low, shoulders slumped, body hunched in defeat. Had she realized how much trouble she was in? Was she guilty? Or was she mourning her friend?

I arrived at the station just in time and was ushered into a small room. We watched the video link-up as D. S. Dave Smith introduced himself to Vanessa and her brief, Jon Hilton. He cut to the chase. "When you threw the ashtray at Mrs. Sheila Brace, did you intend her harm?"

"Of course, I didn't!" Vanessa hissed, shocked. "I loved – love Sheila. She was my best friend, and I didn't throw it at her, I threw it at the bloody wall." She dabbed her heavily made-up eyes with a tissue. "The mirror on the wall behind her was smashed by the ashtray and shards of glass flew everywhere. That's why we didn't know what was wrong with Sheila until we went to help her, but, oh my God, I didn't mean to kill her."

"What happened next?"

"Everything was quiet. Sheila stopped shouting and looked startled. Her eyes widened in shock as colour drained from her face. Then she sort of slumped into her seat and fell sideways onto the floor." She paused, and then went on. "Then I heard someone say, 'What the hell happened, is she alright?' and Barbara said, 'Bloody hell, Vanessa, what did you do?' She screamed at Sue to call an ambulance. I had tried to help Sheila. When we went around the table to where she was lying, we saw what had happened. Then we saw the blood."

D. C. Edwards offered Vanessa a clean tissue from the box on the table and Vanessa blew loudly into it. "I'm quite used to blood because I used to be a nurse, but this was my very dear friend."

"What exactly did you do to help your friend, Ms. Jones?"

"I saw this huge piece of glass sticking out of her. I pulled it out and applied pressure to the wound. I stayed like that until the ambulance came but it was too late. I could see she was slipping away."

Vanessa lost all control then and cried openly until she was all cried out. D. C. Edwards poured a glass of water from the pitcher and handed it to Vanessa, who grasped it tightly and sipped from it.

"What were you and Sheila arguing about?" The detective asked.

"She was calling me names of all sorts."

"Yes, but what started it all, Ms. Jones?"

"She called me a tart and said that I paraded my body to attract men. Sheila had always been jealous because I was the prettier one, even when we were young. Sheila was shy, quiet, and didn't have many boyfriends. She did alright with Simon."

The officers looked at each other again and D. S. Smith asked, "Did Sheila accuse you of sleeping with her husband?"

"Yes, she did," replied Vanessa, "among others."

"Did you?"

Jon Hilton leaned in toward the tape machine and said, "My client has no further comment." Dave Smith grinned sideways towards the two-way mirror at that and told Vanessa Jones, "That's all, Miss."

I went through a myriad of thoughts as I listened to Vanessa's statement. On one hand, she appeared terribly upset about the loss of her friend, yet she was unflustered during questioning. This one was difficult to read. Vanessa was allowed to leave with the instruction to remain close-by, in case further questions arose.

The following morning, I was mulling over the possibilities when Dave Smith called. "Hi, what's happening?" I asked. "We're about to interview Mrs. Barbara Trent, the third witness in the Bridge Case. I thought you might be interested." I certainly was. After thanking and telling Dave I wouldn't miss it, I hung up.

It was anticipated that Barbara would fill in the blanks as to what had taken place at her house that afternoon. Facing the mirror sat Barbara, a mousy-looking woman. Her hair was salt and pepper; she wore a grey corduroy skirt and a grey cardigan. She had obviously taken little care of her appearance for a long time, and it showed. But her blue eyes, bright and clear, were almost too lovely for a woman otherwise so dowdy and of that age.

She shuffled in her seat as if uncomfortable, and constantly wrung her hands, and when asked to give her name and address, she cleared her throat and spoke in a timid voice. D. S. Smith switched the tape on and began.

"Could you tell us why you and three other women were gathered in your dining room on the 26th, Ms. Trent?"

"Yes, yes, of course. We were about to play bridge."

"Was this a regular arrangement?"

"Yes it was, we played bridge roughly twice a month, but we took it in turns to host."

"I see, and it was your turn on the 26th?"

"That's right."

"Do you remember what Vanessa and Sheila were arguing about?"

"Sheila was accusing Vanessa of sleeping with her husband. We all knew that Vanessa was fancied by men, but it was outrageous to accuse her of being involved with Simon. The row escalated quickly and became a horrible cursing match."

Barbara leaned into the table a tiny bit as she almost whispered,

"And then, out of nowhere, Vanessa reached for the heavy ashtray that I kept on the sideboard and she threw it with such force that I thought it might kill Sheila if it were to hit her."

"She was very angry, then?"

"Oh, yes. I don't think I've ever seen her so angry, but so was Sheila, who said, 'I know it's true, Vanessa, he told me everything.' And that's when she called Vanessa a trollop and said that she ought to act her age and leave other people's husbands alone."

"Do you believe that she was trying to hit Sheila with the ashtray?"

"I really couldn't say."

"After you discovered what had happened, did you think that Ms. Jones was trying to save Sheila before the ambulance arrived?"

"I thought so, her being a nurse after all. You'd expect that she'd know what to do, but I have wondered since – why didn't she try to resuscitate Sheila? Then again, I suppose it was all very sudden. Vanessa just sat there with Sheila's head on her lap, rocking to and fro. She was sobbing silently I remember, not making a sound but big fat tears fell from her face onto Sheila's. And then, when the paramedics arrived, they had to pull her away."

It was clear that D. S. Smith and I were on the same page. Surely a nurse, who had only retired some seven years ago, would know that one shouldn't remove anything from a wound until the patient has been taken to the hospital? Otherwise, the wound would very likely bleed out.

What I needed to think about was this – did Vanessa act appropriately? Why *didn't* she practice CPR on Sheila? She didn't even put her into the recovery position, check her airway or cover her as she waited for the ambulance. Plus, if Vanessa had really tried to stop the bleeding, she would have turned Sheila onto her front in order to apply enough pressure to the wound, and she would surely have called for towels or something to use to stop the bleeding. Oversight or malice? I wondered.

I woke early the next morning, the bright sun casting beautiful patterns of light around the room as the rays bounced off a crystal vase which stood on the windowsill. I was just thinking about getting out of bed when my phone rang. It was D. S. Smith.

"Good morning, Maria. I have news for you. The coroner just called, and he's ordered a post-mortem. Oh, and I spoke to Simon Brace yesterday; he's a smarmy git and thinks this case has nothing to do with him. I don't think he even knew about the argument. He told me the marriage was long dead."

"Did you ask him about the affair?"

"Asked him outright; got a straight answer. He told me they'd been at it for years, casually. He said he had no intention of leaving his wife. And get this: Sheila had been suspicious and confronted him just last weekend. He, of course, denied it. It doesn't really help us a lot. It all hangs on the coroner really, and the post-mortem results. We should hear something in a couple of days and then we can decide which way to jump," he finished.

"Okay, that's great, thanks for letting me know."

"No problem, I'll leave you with your coffee now."

I was surprised about the post-mortem request. It was pretty obvious to us all what had killed Sheila, but I guessed the coroner needed to know exactly how the glass had caused her death, and perhaps, like Dave and me, he wondered if Vanessa could have saved her – and whether removing the glass had actually caused her demise.

***

It was raining heavily on Monday morning as I ran from the car to the front door of the station and almost collided with Joanne Edwards. The tall, dark-haired detective constable informed me that Dave had received a call from the coroner at the crack of dawn telling him that the report was complete and had brought up some surprises. Shaking our coats free from rainwater, we stepped into the lift.

"The D. S. called this morning and asked me to meet him at the coroner's office. He's gone back to question Simon Brace, Sheila's husband," she said.

"I'm intrigued, now more than ever."

"Let's wait for the boss, but you can read the report yourself while we do."

That was exactly what I did as I waited for Dave's return about an hour later. Joanne had not exaggerated – the post-mortem report did, indeed, prove interesting. D. S. Smith greeted me with a warm hug as he joined me in his office. He seemed cheerful for a Monday as he sat down, called for some coffee, and faced me across the desk.

"Well?" he asked, "Bit of a turn-up! Puts a different spin on things, eh?"

"It did take me by surprise!" I replied.

Although the report stated that Sheila Brace had died from 'blood loss following the incision of a glass shard of about seven inches in length into the renal artery, causing shock and loss of kidney function', the surprise element was a malignant brain tumour, which was, according to our pathologist, terminal and metastasized to several areas of the body. In short, Sheila Brace had but a short time to live.

Dave had naturally requested an interview with Simon to gauge whether he was aware of her condition. It appeared that he wasn't, and according to Dave, he exhibited some vestige of humanity and sorrow at the news. Indeed, he collapsed in shock and was carried by ambulance to the hospital complaining of chest pains.

It seemed that Sheila hadn't told her husband about her illness and although genuinely saddened at what he was told, we would never know if the knowledge might have changed his relationship with his wife.

"I want to get Vanessa Jones back in. Let's find out what she knew," Dave said, "I've got a funny feeling that she won't be surprised by the news." D. S. Smith dispatched a car to collect Vanessa and she was in the interview room within the hour. She waived the right to counsel and the interview began. The detective leaned across the table, looked straight into Vanessa's eyes, and asked, "Were you aware that Sheila was dying from Glioblastoma Multiforme?"

Vanessa remained composed as she told him, "Of course I knew, Sergeant. I was her best friend, practically her only friend in the whole world. I was the one who took her to the hospital the day she learned about her diagnosis. I was with her when she was told that she had weeks to live, and I helped keep her secret, especially from Simon."

"Why did she want to keep her illness from people?"

"She thought they would try to make her have futile treatment. She was dying and she wanted — rather needed to die with dignity. The only thing she worried about was the pain. People noticed that she sometimes acted strangely, but it was reasoned down to age. And that's how we kept her secret."

"But the end came sooner than either of you expected," concluded the somewhat subdued Joanne.

"Did Sheila say anything to you before she died?" asked Smith.

"Yes. She thanked me."

***

Although the post-mortem had shown that Sheila died from shock due to blood loss and trauma to her body, the coroner was not confident enough to hang his hat on a cause of death any more than the police or the CPS was. A date was set for the inquest.

I was still troubled by Vanessa's story. Given the fact that she had practically confessed to allowing (even aiding) Sheila to bleed to death, I still wasn't convinced of her motive. On the surface, what she did would appear to be a kind gesture to let her friend slip away peacefully. Yet, the law was there to ensure that people do not act like God. Even so, Vanessa could not have anticipated the turn of events that had led to Sheila's death. Was she, therefore, responsible?

A few weeks later, I received an email from the coroner. The inquest had thoroughly investigated the case. A transcript of the hearing was attached, and I opened it eagerly. The post-mortem report showed that the injury to Sheila's body was the reason she had died. Vanessa had faced a few probing questions concerning her relationship with Sheila and Simon Brace, both of whom she described as 'very close friends'.

Supported by the evidence of the other witnesses, Vanessa's explanation of how she had thrown the ashtray at the wall was accepted.

In summing up, the judge expressed his sympathy to the family and added that he would have been satisfied with a verdict of accidental death. However, on reflection, he said, "The act of throwing the heavy object had not been an accident; it was a considered action." The entire courtroom held its breath as he continued, "but, the ashtray did not kill the victim. It was, as we now know a shard of broken glass which did the damage and I do not believe that anyone could have anticipated what happened thereafter." The judge returned a verdict of death by misadventure. There was nothing more for me to do then but officially withdraw from the case and the investigation was closed.

It was a couple of months later while sharing a nice bottle of house red with Dave Smith when I voiced out my feelings of restlessness. "You know what?" said Dave, "We have to write this one off. You were never going to get a prosecution out of this case. For whatever reason Vanessa Jones allowed her friend to die, you need to remember the outcome was always going to be the same for Sheila Brace – a peaceful and pain-free death."

Dave was right of course, and it was that thought that helped me sleep at night.

3

STRANGER

by Prajwal Shukla

Daniel agreed to join Mr. and Mrs. Vendetta that weekend to attend their daughter's dance recital. He asked if he could find a seat on such short notice, to which Mr. Vendetta responded, "Of course you will, Daniel. We own the school."

Daniel obliged. That weekend, he accompanied the couple to watch Miss Beaguette's performance. They were so intrinsically proud of her. Although Daniel wasn't interested, he was stumped by the performance, so much that he sprang from his seat along with the others.

The couple then invited Daniel along to meet the school's dance trainer, an awardee on a national television show and featured in over twelve magazines for her talent. Daniel went backstage and fell in love with Lily as soon as their eyes met.

Daniel was lucky enough to get the opportunity to talk to her while Mr. and Mrs. V were busy appreciating their daughter. He used that chance and asked her out on a date, which she accepted. Thus, after a quick bite, Daniel walked her home that night. He soon realised that he couldn't keep away and wanted to meet her again.

For their second date, they went out for a fulfilling Sunday brunch and found out that their parents were from the same city. A few weeks later, Lily booked them a show to the movie Daniel had been desperately waiting for. That was when it became clear to Daniel that she had feelings for him as much as he did for her.

After one of their dates, late at night, they stood outside her door. Daniel drew her in towards him as he looked right into her eyes, and then kissed her with so much passion that it put the moon to shame. He flashed her a boyish grin and walked away into the darkness, leaving a blushing and grinning Lily on the doorstep. He didn't realise he was being followed until a black, unmarked van pulled over right beside him, and two people grabbed him in.

"What the hell, Miguel? Someone could've seen us," Daniel snapped.

"What are you doing? She isn't a part of the assignment," Miguel shot back, irritated.

"You better have a good reason for doing this," said Daniel.

"We found another one."

Daniel silently gazed out the window. Another teenager had been murdered the same way. And just like before, the autopsy had revealed almost invisible traces of the same drug.

He had to get to the bottom of this.

***

Michelle, Daniel's other partner, insisted on being in touch with Daniel through his earpiece every time he was near Mr. Vendetta. She tracked everything in real-time and made sure everything went as per plan as their assignment was about to end in just four days. Daniel had to be on tiptoes.

Meanwhile, the more his affection for Lily grew, the more he got worried about her safety. He started having recurring nightmares where he would go home only to find his secret wardrobe unlocked, with Lily being held at gunpoint and tied up with her arms cuffed to the chair. She would look at him, her eyes pleading for help and her agony indescribable. A masked man would shoot her in the head and Daniel would wake up, startled.

One morning, after another of these nightmares, Michelle found him drooling in sleep at his work desk at 8 in the morning. Roughly shaking him by the shoulder, she reminded him that he is needed at the office. Mr. Vendetta was suspected to have a confidential meeting. Daniel showered hastily and darted right out towards Mr. V's office.

"Hello Mr. Vendetta," he said, fighting to catch his breath.

Mr. Vendetta looked at him suspiciously. "Where have you been Daniel? You're unusually late today." Daniel voiced out his apology, but Mr. Vendetta seemed too buoyant to be disappointed.

"Anyway, let's get down to business. You've been quite helpful to me, Daniel. You've been loyal to my family and my company. Beaguette really likes you as well. I can't thank you enough for keeping my wife busy at her kitties and you've managed to impress me more than anyone ever has."

"I don't know what to say. Thank you, Mr. Vendetta."

Mr. V clapped his shoulder jubilantly. "I'm happy to have you. Alright then, Daniel, can I trust you with something? I see some great potential in you to be a great addition to my board of directors – a committee if you will, for operations that are in a direct conflict with the intention of International authorities." Daniel stared back, his face impassive. "Can I?" Mr. Vendetta stressed.

"Yes, Mr. V. Absolutely," said Daniel.

"The board makes some confidential transactions, and we've been doing it all on an analogue system with very few people involved. I need you to set up a digital system for us to carry out this process with the highest security, without making too much noise."

Mr. V was quite vulnerable at this point and this was the moment Daniel needed. "I'll see that it's done, sir," said Daniel and strode out of the cabin. Pressing his earpiece, he murmured, "Team Beta, fall back. The mission is a no-go."

Daniel had expected to catch Mr. V with his lies and hunt down the rest, but he was directly being invited to the lion's cave. This was the perfect chance to bring down the whole group of elite who ran the drug cartel and were responsible for the murders of innocent teenagers.

Michelle, Miguel, and Daniel arranged a meeting with their boss. "This is merely a crack in the window. With the right way, the window would open big and wide." Their boss agreed. Daniel would meet the board the next day, with a team standing by for orders to arrest them.

As per the plan, Daniel was prepared with back-up for the meeting Mr. V had arranged. With the mansion surrounded at 100 meters distance from all sides, Mr. V took him to his basement. All signals were jammed, the room was secured by four guards on each side of the hallway, biometric scanners, A.I. motion detectors, and a voice pattern analyser.

Daniel entered the room along with Mr. V to find seven chairs at a huge table shaped in a V. The head seat of the V belonged to Mr. Vendetta and right behind it stood a gentleman wearing a 5-piece suit, almost 60, with long salt and pepper hair and a goatee. He wore a huge ruby-studded, eye-blinding ring in the index finger of his right hand and walked with the support of a cane. Mr. V introduced him as Mr. Deckard Halt. Daniel shook hands with the man.

Mr. Halt offered Daniel a drink as Mr. V said, "I'll let you two acquaint, don't mind me." Mr. Halt asked about Daniel's past and how he got here. He told Daniel that he had moved countries and had a family here a long time ago. His wife had passed in a gang war, which came off as an accident to the world, and there was no trace of his four-year-old son, Danny, leaving Halt to assume the worst.

Daniel began to perspire. He was four when his mom had passed away in an accident which hardly seemed like one, and his father had been next to impossible. "You have your father's eyes," his mother had said, "And you two funnily have an identical mole behind your right ear."

"Daniel! Are you listening?" asked Mr. Halt.

Daniel wasn't, not when he was staring right into a pair of eyes bearing the same shade as his — bright blue with a slight tinge of navy. Could it really be? Just then, Mr. Halt tilted his neck to his left, giving Daniel a crystal-clear view. A mole identical to Daniel's nestled behind Halt's right ear, just near the lobe.

Daniel couldn't breathe. Not only was Deckard Halt his father, but he was one of the masterminds behind this awful drug that was killing so many. He wanted to walk away, but he had no time to let his emotions take over.

Soon enough, the rest of the seven arrived. The meeting would be followed by lunch and last about three hours. Daniel's team was instructed to infiltrate the mansion if there was no response from Daniel within that time. Mr. V introduced Daniel to all of the board members and informed him what his job would be. Mr. Halt and the others asked him questions, which Daniel dutifully clarified. Just when Daniel wondered if that was it, Mr. V announced, "Zed wants to talk." He switched the audio on. Daniel figured that Zed was their boss.

After a brief introduction of Daniel, and zero traces of suspicion, they got to the point. Magician's Cape, a drug illegally and rarely acquired, had been tested on and had killed many teenagers due to overdose. Daniel's mind went back to the two murdered boys. Dealers were selling it as a psychedelic without informing about the harm of overconsumption, and addicts who OD'd on it ended up losing their lives.

"Ulrich isn't backing down. He wants the deal at fifty thousand –" Mr. V was saying.

"Not a cent below seventy-five," snarled Zed.

Daniel could feel the trickle of sweat down his temple. This was it. He checked the time. It had been well past three hours. Michelle and Miguel would be here any minute now. Just as everyone was about to take a lunch break, the doors burst open, revealing Daniel's team. Outnumbered and caught off guard, the seven didn't get much time to react as Daniel and the others got a hold of them.

"You are under arrest for dealing drugs and causing the deaths of over five hundred people," Daniel stated, having used the distraction to pin Halt's hands behind his back. His conflict of emotions was surfacing, and he felt he might break, but kept up the façade.

All seven dealers of The Magician's Cape were put in a van to be taken to the headquarters. Mr. Halt had been looking at Daniel foully ever since the revelation of who he was, voicing out profanities.

As Daniel thrust him into one of the vans, he said icily, "You know, it's funny. My mother also passed away in an 'accident' when I was four and I grew up without a father. I have a blurry memory of him calling me Danny. My mother told me that my eyes reminded her of him, and that there is a mole behind my ear which marks my resemblance to him." Halt squinted his eyes at Daniel in confusion. Daniel tilted his neck to his left, pointing to his own mole.

As realisation hit Halt, he slammed the door and watched the van speed away. He tried ignoring the turmoil in his stomach. Only he knew how difficult that had been for him.

He thought of Lily and it made him smile. Suddenly, he missed her. Dialling her number, he waited for her to answer. When she did, his smile widened.

"What are you doing this weekend?" asked Daniel.

"Nothing, why?"

"Pack your bags. It's time to ride into the sunset."

4

A DAUGHTER'S PLIGHT

by Yashika Rawal

*T*oday *is an unusual day. The typical flurry of activity at the railway station seems missing. The few people who exist are in their own world.*

A man is kneeling in front of a little girl of five. He is wearing torn khaki pants and a maroon sweater. His torn pants and his dishevelled hair are giving him the look of a wandering beggar. His face is smeared with tears and there is a deep cut near his left eyebrow with blood seeping through it. The girl is facing her father, but her face is not clear. Judging by her clothes, no one will believe that she can be his daughter. While the man's face is covered with dirt, her face radiates nothing but purity.

"But Papa, you promised you won't leave me," complains the girl in a small voice.

"I will always be with you, Ridhu," he replies, wiping the tears from her face, "This world is cruel. It is not for good people. But remember, God always ensures justice..."

Panting, I jolt up from my restless slumber. My heart rate has sped up, my head is throbbing, and my clothes are damp from all the sweat. I rub my cheeks and close my eyes tightly. Swallowing hard, I clutch furiously at my chest, hoping my heartbeats would slow down. With a sigh, I keep my cold feet down the couch, wear my slippers and head out to the bridge over the river. The loud sound of ripples calms my mind every time.

Just two days ago, I had been the happiest person on earth. I was finally about to get what I wanted. Around six in the evening, I arrived at my apartment in search for the keys and opened the door only to find Raunak sitting awkwardly on my couch.

"What the heck?" I cried, entering my living room. Raunak was my best friend, rather the only friend in my life. But more than just my friend, he was also the son of the man who'd driven my father to suicide.

Around twenty years ago, Dad had been giddy with excitement about his new chemical workshop. He'd told me, "Uncle Mahajan is my partner!" But he was unaware of a new crime being woven.

Mahajan and I had never met, so he didn't know that I was the daughter of his prey. My father, in an attempt to hide me from Mahajan's manslaughter, took me to my aunt's and left me there with the promise to never leave. He kept his promise. He is with me, albeit not physically. He's there in my heart and my dreams.

"Earth to Ridhima," Raunak interrupted my thoughts.

I scowled, "Why are you here at my place? I gave you a bunch of spare keys only in case of an emergency."

"Relax! Why are you so feisty today? Is there something I should know?" he smirked and wiggled his eyebrows, teasing me. I poured myself a glass of water and looked up at him. He stood there, just staring at me.

"What? Do you want some?" I said.

He shook his head no. "I just want some help."

"Nope, I'm not helping you," I declared.

He ignored me and chuckled, "You know how I always tell you that you should join me at my father's chemical factory, don't you? I know your obsession with chemicals."

"Okay, what's the catch?"

"Okay, so there's a company dealing with us. They want to do some experimentation with sulphuric acid. If I make it work, my dad will finally believe in me."

"So, you want me to help you in experimenting."

"Bingo."

"Stupid, stupid idea. I just have an interest, but I'm not a professional. That's too dangerous."

"Believe me, nothing would happen."

I relented. "Fine."

"Did you just agree? I spent hours on a speech to convince you," he pouted dramatically. I shrugged, bored.

"There's one more thing," he said. I lifted my eyebrows questioningly.

He sighed heavily, "No one should know that you helped me, especially my father. This is my only opportunity to prove myself. Please? This will be the last time I ask for a favour." Yes. That would be the last time for Raunak. Just like there had been a last time for my father. I felt tears pricking at the corner of my eyes.

Raunak must have thought I was ogling at him. Giving me a shy smile, he said, "I believe you're the best at what you do, and this time, too, you'll nail it."

I swallowed the lump in my throat and replied, keeping my excitement in check, "Fine."

He came and hugged me tightly. If my arms would've been strong like his, I would have strangled him a long time ago.

"You're sure you will do it?"

"Yes, I have to. Last time, right?

"Okay! See you tomorrow then."

It oddly felt like we were on the same page, talking about my revenge instead of his plan. He was almost near the door when I stopped him. He turned.

"Thanks for stopping by," I simply said.

He just winked and left with a goofy grin.

That night, I slept wonderfully after a lot of sleepless nights. My dad must also have spent many sleepless nights. Could he have ended his life to not get stuck in this nightmare? No, he wasn't a coward. Not the man who taught me to be strong.

I could've ended the life of the man responsible for my dad's death, but death wouldn't have make him feel the pain. His death would free his soul, but the loss of his own flesh would definitely make him feel the way I did. I wanted him to feel pain.

The death of my friend would end my miseries, I'd thought.

Yesterday, with that hope, I went to his chemical workshop. As expected, no one came to know. Raunak had turned the CCTV surveillance off. He was a true friend; he was helping me even during his last moments.

After around two hours of helping him, I added the wrong chemicals to create an explosion. It was easy. I exited the workshop, leaving him alone, waiting for death. I rushed towards my apartment without taking a look behind. Why look back when a beautiful future awaited me with open arms? At least that's what I believed. After getting myself in, I locked my apartment, picked my phone, and frantically dialled him to cross-check my plan's success.

"The person you are trying to call is currently unreachable," I could hear. Relief spread through me. He was dead, and now,

I could live. I settled myself in bed. Suddenly, my phone rang. I sprang out of bed after seeing the caller id, 'Raunak'.

I closed my eyes for a split moment. How could this be happening? Hitting answer, I put it up against my ear. An unknown voice on the other side stated, "Your number had been the most recently dialled from this phone. Its owner, a boy, has died in a fire accident."

Of course, I knew that. But why wasn't I feeling relieved anymore? Tears were rolling down my cheeks unannounced. I felt sick. I felt a lot of pain. That pain could not make him return and that made things worse.

The clock ticked loudly that night. I knew I had waited for this since eternity. I had to go and see the suffering of Raunak's father. But my limbs were paralysed. I was alone, yet again.

Hours later, I decided to go to Raunak's house to confess my real identity. I played the conversation in my head, "I'm Ridhima, your best friend's daughter. The friend you murdered, remember?"

The drive to his house felt too long that day. The surroundings were a blur. My mind was hazed by Raunak's thoughts. Finally, the house came into view. A huge crowd had filled his house. I was there to see Mr. Mahajan, but I caught myself subconsciously searching for Raunak.

Gathering courage, I went to meet my dad's culprit. That poor soul had refused to meet anyone and had locked himself inside. I wasn't going to sit and mourn. In the hall was a portrait of my handsome friend, sans corpse. The body must have melted from the burning chemicals. The thought made me cringe.

My friend's life hadn't been too long, but it had definitely been big. He had earned all these people's love who were mourning him. I wouldn't mourn even my own passing. I sprinted towards my car to exit the place as fast as my legs could take me. Later, I got the news that Raunak's father was hospitalised due to cardiac arrest. I tossed and turned in bed that night till I could feel the sun peeping through the curtains. I lay there for some more time.

This noon, I went to my living room with a bottle of sleeping pills. I sat on the same couch my friend had sat on just two days ago, when I felt the rustling of a paper under the seat. I stopped breathing when I saw what it was – a letter in Raunak's handwriting. At the age of ten, I had found my dad's letter and now, this. Two things were common in both of them: they weren't letters, they were suicide notes. While my dad's letter had filled me with rage, my friend's filled me with regret. Now, I am here at this bridge, alone, the sound of the ripples failing to calm my nerves.

Raunak had somehow managed to know about my evil side. He must've read my diary that day. He wanted me to be happy, even if it could only be brought by his sacrifice. But now, all I could feel was guilt. He intentionally asked for my help. He wanted his father to feel bad for what he did. I read and reread that letter at least ten times.

The last lines of his letter mentioned, *"I know I'll be gone by the time you read this. You are the best at what you do, and if you've decided to do this, then you will succeed. I know you're smart, but this time, I outsmarted you, my friend."* I could feel the hair behind my neck rising and a chill ran down my spine. The point in my conversation with him where I felt we were on the same page, we actually were. I could recall every hint – about my secret being spilled out, if I were sure about my actions and also at the end, near the door, when he winked and smirked. He put himself in death's path so I could kill him.

I fall to my knees on the bridge, howling. My friend is gone.

My dad was right. This world isn't for good people. This is hell. Good people like my father and Raunak are where they are meant to be. My dad's murderer and I are here, where we belong. "I am sorry, papa, your daughter isn't like you. She is just like your killer." Today, out of all the other days, I feel like he can hear me. "Dad, my mind couldn't think of anything beyond revenge. Just like a pair of handcuffs restrain the movement of a pair of hands, my mind was restrained by the rage boiled up within me. Tomorrow, I shall surrender myself. Please, please take care of my friend."

With that, I lie on the bridge. A raindrop falls over my cheek, making me wonder if my dad must be crying over my fate and what I have made of myself. I decide to give a final look to the skies above before whispering, "Goodbye, Dad and Raunak, I'll miss you."

5

Sugar, Spice... But Not Everything Nice

by Saloni Wagle

Arianna Beckson stood outside her bakery, "Sugar and Spice" at four o'clock, impervious to the chilly breeze of the early morning. There was a malicious smirk on her face. And why wouldn't there be? She had waited a whole year for the day when she would meet her next 'The One'.

Every year, she would design a new ploy to meet him, or her. This year, it was going to be cherry almond tartlets, one of them being a 'special treat'. Before entering her kitchen, she rummaged her tote to make sure she had the packet – her special ingredient.

Ten minutes later, Arianna was emptying the cans of pitted cherries into the mixing bowl. She was going to have to make the filling, knead the pastry dough and bake the tartlets, all by herself, before her staff started coming in at five o'clock. But she knew it was all going to be worth it.

It was almost ten minutes to five by the time she had rolled and cut the dough, pressing the circles meticulously into the tartlet tins. She then filled the tins with the cherry almond filling. All the tins, except one.

For the last 'special' tartlet, Arianna mixed in some cherry pits. She then added the white, powdery contents of the packet and some extra sugar to the filling. After giving it a nice stir, she filled the last tartlet tin with it, and placed them all in the oven, setting the timer to forty minutes. Arianna smiled. Now, all she had to do was loiter around till nine when the bakery would open and wait for her 'lucky' customer.

By half-past nine, the bakery was buzzing with customers. From the payment counter, Arianna could see some familiar faces. Tony, the 10-year-old kid, who would stop by every Saturday for a strawberry muffin. Gina, the chic girl from uptown, who enjoyed sipping her soymilk latte before heading off to work. There was also the old man, who came in from time to time for a bear claw, and in some strange way, reminded Arianna of her grandfather. She didn't know his name but liked the guy and kind of hoped he wouldn't be the lucky one today. Yet, there was a part of her that wondered how he would look if he 'won the prize'.

There were some new people in as well. Arianna observed them keenly. A gothic girl, waiting at the artisan bread counter for her ham and cheese sourdough sandwich. A man in tweed – probably a professor, deciding which coffee to have. There was also a couple sitting by the window, eating donuts off each other's hands. "It should be them," Arianna thought to herself, irked by their flirtation.

"Here goes your first tartlet of the day!"

Mimi's voice brought Arianna back from her contemplation. She looked at the customer her waitress was pointing at. It was a suave-looking young man, dressed sharply in a navy blue slim-fit suit. He was sitting at the corner table, reading a Forbes magazine. Arianna instantly knew he had to be the one.

Mimi was about to take a random tartlet from the display counter when Arianna stopped her. "Let me," she said, deliberately picking up the piece in the bottom corner of the board, and Mimi gladly obliged.

She placed her special tartlet on a serving tray, with a spoon and some paper napkins, and walked towards her lucky customer. As she came near his table, he looked up at her and smiled politely. Arianna's heart skipped a beat. The maturity in his blue eyes flattered the boyishness in his smile and his rugged beard. Arianna smiled back.

"First time here?" she asked, as she set down the tray in front of him.

"Oh, yeah," he replied, "Hi, I'm Dave." Arianna loved it when they were chatty.

"Arianna," she said, giving Dave her most charming smile. "You are indeed lucky, Mr. Dave. Not many get to taste my special tartlets." Dave seemed a little confused but was too gracious to ask. "Um, thank you. I'll definitely relish it."

Arianna started walking back to her spot. Turning back, she saw Dave eat the first spoonful and instantly felt aroused. Fortunately, she had a good view of Dave from the payment counter. A front-row seat to the live show.

Dave seemed to like the tartlet. The sweetness of cherries balanced out well with the buttery goodness of the crust. He was particularly enjoying the almond bits in the filling. Strangely, these almonds tasted cherry-like. "They must have been incorporated really well," he speculated, as he went in for the last spoonful. But before he could ingest it, something happened - something unlike anything ever before.

Dave couldn't swallow the morsel. He could feel his gullet stiffen and narrow. His body started trembling. He tried to reach for his bottle of water, but it felt almost as if he had no control over his hand. He tried to shout for help, only to find that his throat had dried up. His words barely came out and were completely inaudible. With great effort, he turned his neck around.

Through his blurred vision, he could see Arianna coming towards him. Dave, somehow, pushed himself on his feet to grope her for help. But his legs were shaking uncontrollably, and before he could grasp Arianna, he felt a convulsion in his left leg. The sudden jerk tipped the leg of the table behind him and made him lose his balance. Dave collapsed onto the floor and sensed the table land on his right calf. But amidst the upheaval, he hardly noticed the agony.

He could barely breathe by this point. Gasping for air, Dave tried to stay conscious. There was intense heat around him and he could feel droplets of sweat roll down his forehead. A bright light was hitting him in flashes, and he struggled to keep his eyes open.

'Call…one…" he heard a voice say.

Then everything blacked out and Dave became unnaturally motionless.

Two Days Later

"Did he have any family?" a deeply distressed Arianna Beckson asked, sitting opposite Officer Mendes.

"A wife, two daughters, and an ailing mother."

Officer Mendes pitied this young woman. "It was horrid to see someone die because of something I cooked with so much love," she had said, and the cop could see it in her moist eyes. Leaning forward, he tried to assuage her. "I can understand what you are going through, Miss Beckson. But you have no reason to feel guilty. You didn't leave in the cherry pits. You didn't cause the cyanide poisoning, Ms. Beckson. You are the last person to share the blame of Dave Millers' death, if at all!"

Twenty minutes of reassuring words later, Arianna walked out of the police station, smiling smugly. She had been exceptionally smart this year. 'Cyanide poisoning from cherry pits' was a stroke of absolute genius. She reminisced about the day. Her plan had gone way better than she ever imagined.

Unsuspecting Dave had relished the entire tartlet. Arianna had expected the cyanide to trigger the seizure in just two bites and had started to get anxious when it hadn't. After all, it was the one day in a year, when she allowed herself the pleasure, and she couldn't let it go by vainly.

Just when her doubts had started to creep in, she saw the look on Dave's face change, going straight from indulgence to gagging. Then, there had been just some alarm in his eyes, but Arianna was sure that by the time she was done with him, it would be classic panic and horror. The man had started shaking frighteningly. Seeing that he had gained the attention of other customers, she had realized this was the time to start her act.

"Oh my God!" Shrieking, she had run towards Dave as he was trying to stand up. "Somebody, help!"

But before she could reach him, the spasms had kicked in. Dave had toppled, making her glass table fall on his leg. By then, the waitresses and a few customers had come to help and were lifting the heavy table off his leg. Arianna had kneeled beside her lucky guy and had taken his manicured palm into her own.

"Just breathe…breathe…breathe," she had bolstered him, looking at his handsome, doomed face. She could see the trepidation in his eyes and the perspiration on his forehead. She had felt this elated only after a full year.

"Call 911!" Mimi had shouted desperately. But before anyone could even dial, Dave had suddenly become still. Then, all he had been was a beautiful, lucky corpse lying in her hands, his sea-blue eyes looking up at her with an alluring lifelessness. Dave had undoubtedly been the most charming one yet,

Arianna thought to herself, as she walked down the street from the station.

She had seen Dave's family at his funeral the day before and could fantasize about their lives now. His wife – desolate, struggling to play the roles of both parents. His six and three-year-old kids – growing up without a father. His mother – grief-stricken, waiting to reunite with her son. Arianna felt a wave of gratification. A part of their lives would now be missing. Just like hers was. Forever.

6

THE INTERVIEW

by Srikanth Palaparthy

Melinda lived in an old house near the end of the village. The villagers described her as a sweet old lady who always helped others; always lent money to those in need. Fortune had been kind to her. She had enough money to live decently in the twilight years of her life. Melinda was the perfect subject for Krishna's YouTube series. He had interviewed over twenty old men and women for his series, 'Experiences'. This was going to be his final interview before he went back home.

He'd heard from a talkative old lady that Melinda had been orphaned at birth. She had also seen the murder of her adopted parents when she was only seventeen. This intrigued Krishna. He couldn't wait to meet Melinda and tell her story to the world.

Arriving at the house, Krishna felt that 'old' couldn't even begin to describe it. The tiled roof couldn't wait to hug the ground with the walls damp and black. The house had only three rooms. An old woman was sitting on a wheelchair in the middle of the living room, engrossed in her knitting. The TV was on, playing a movie to the walls of the house.

"It's embroidery. I'm trying to knit a bird on this white cloth," Melinda said to Krishna without looking up.

"Glad to know that I don't have to shout," Krishna remarked, "And that looks beautiful," he added, noticing the embroidery.

"Thank you," said Melinda, "I don't have men visiting me anymore. It's all old women who need an ear for gossip. So, may I know the purpose of your visit?"

"Well, ma'am, my name is Krishna. I enable senior citizens to share their wisdom with the world through my YouTube channel."

"So you make money off of other people's lives."

"Yeah, I guess so but –" Krishna started.

"Not that there's anything wrong with it," Melinda added quickly.

"Yeah, I was going to say that at least I give a voice to people instead of suppressing it," said Krishna.

Melinda looked up at Krishna for the first time that evening. The man with a low raspy voice of a smoker looked like one too. "You need to stop smoking, young man. It's making you look older than you are," she said.

"I know, ma'am. I'm trying to cut down. There's something else that calms me down now."

"Oh, what's that?" Melinda asked.

Krishna did not answer. He stood there, fidgeting with his microphone wires, which he had taken out of his bag. "Where are my manners? I haven't even offered you a drink. Tea? Coffee?" Melinda asked, breaking the awkward silence that had filled the air.

"That won't be necessary. Let's start the interview. It's getting late already," Krishna said.

"No, No, I'll get you something," Melinda said. She stood up and walked into the kitchen, which was opposite the main door.

She can walk, Krishna thought, as he busied himself setting up the interview equipment. There was an old, creaky wooden chair in a corner. Krishna was afraid that it'd collapse mid-interview, so he decided against using it. Melinda came out of the kitchen with two cups of coffee. Krishna sat on the ground beside the wheelchair, while asking her to sit on the wheelchair. Through the camera lens, it looked like an old woman was sitting with her grandson, telling him about her long and arduous journey through life. Melinda then started to narrate the events of the day on which her parents died.

"It seemed that the heavens had opened up that day, as if to let my parents' souls inside. I woke up earlier than usual, at six o'clock. Mother and I loved dancing in the rain. I walked into the kitchen, searching for her, but did not find her there. Everything was quiet, except for the soft patter of the rain. There was a slight stench of death in the air. I walked around the house looking for my mother and came to a stop outside my parents' room. My heart thundering against my chest, I opened the door. The image of the bedroom that day will be etched into my brain forever.

"Mother and Father on their bed – the white sheets covered in their blood. Their white clothes turned red. The smell – ugh, the smell. I ran out of the house and puked. We didn't have phones in those days. I ran to the police station in the state I'd woken up. There was no one there, except for a constable. There, I waited for two hours, and only returned to the house with the police. I was scared to go in alone. The case itself took more than a month to solve and catch the culprit.

"He was a close friend of my father and had his eye on my mother for a while. I had noticed it before, but my mother being as naive as she was, ignored my warnings. She offered to give private classes to his daughter at our house. He always accompanied his daughter to these classes. The day before the murder, my father was supposed to go to the city for some work. His friend took this opportunity and came to our house after I fell asleep. He started to force himself on my mother and dragged her into her bedroom.

"Father missed his bus to the city and thus returned home. He heard my mother screaming and ran inside the house to find his close friend on top of his wife. In the commotion that followed, both my parents were murdered. The murderer then placed the bodies beside each other and stole some gold and cash to make it look like a robbery gone wrong. The whole month and a half, which is how long it took to solve and convict the culprit, was a nightmare for me. Shortly after that, I left the village in search of work."

Melinda ended her story in tears. The recollection of the events had shaken her up. She could feel her heart racing. Krishna saw her wipe the sweat off her brow.

"You're a very heavy sleeper, huh?" he said, standing up.

"What?" she asked, looking confused.

"I mean, your father heard your mother screaming from outside the house, while you slept in the other room like a log. Also, why didn't the neighbours come to help if she was screaming?"

"I-I am a he-heavy sleeper. Daniel always said so. I don't know about the neighbours."

"Hmm, they were heavy sleepers too, I guess," Krishna mocked. "It's funny. You know, this is the second time I'm hearing this story in my series."

"What? You've interviewed someone before who told you the same story?"

"Yes, an old man. A surprisingly hale-looking old man. He was ten years older than you, in his nineties. He told the same story as you. After some further probing, though, his story drastically changed. I came to this village looking for you right after his interview. He was none other than the cop who solved the double murder. He was in touch with you for years after the case, wasn't he? I mean, he was the one that gave me your address. Do you want to know the story he told me, Srilekha?" asked Krishna.

He was now standing with his bag in his hands. The camera was turned off and taken down from its pedestal. Melinda had started to sweat profusely after hearing her maiden name. It was almost a lifetime since anyone called her by that name.

"How do you…" she trailed off. Words were at the edge of her tongue, but the strength to speak eluded her. Krishna pulled out a severed head from his bag, cabinet-sized, and placed it in front of her. It was the lone constable who had been at the station that night.

"Try and lie now, bitch," Krishna snarled. He was standing behind the head. Melinda noticed a sharp sickle in his left hand. She looked up at Krishna with a terrified expression. Her heart was beating out of her chest now.

"It was you and he that framed my great grandfather for the murders. It was because of you that my grandmother turned into a sex worker. It was because of you that my mother and sister became sex workers, too. All because your father caught you in bed, sleeping with your mother!" Krishna's voice gradually increased from being gravely still to an unbearable, murderous scream. Melinda was horrified. She started to say something but stopped.

"Yes, I know," continued Krishna. "The lady running the brothel now is my grandmother's best friend. She gave me a lead on what had happened all those years ago. I followed the trail of breadcrumbs, unravelling the whole tale. My grandmother saw you take your mother into your room during a class. Sometime later, your mother came out crying, adjusting her hair and saree. She apologized to my grandmother, asking her to leave. This started happening a lot.

"My grandmother even saw you two kissing once. You were the one forcing yourself on your mother. You were the one caught by your father. You killed him and couldn't bear it when your mom started attacking you for killing him, so you killed her, too. You then ran to the police station, not knowing what you were doing. The constable knew you well and he agreed to help you, on the condition that you sleep with him. You agreed and my great grandfather became an easy scapegoat. You ruined my life, and now, Srilekha, the day of reckoning is upon you."

"I-I didn't know, I'm sorry," Melinda murmured.

"Sorry won't cut it!" Krishna thundered, kicking the head out of the way. Melinda threw her empty cup at him in a desperate attempt to save her life, but the young man's reflexes were quick. He moved to the left, dodging the cup, and caught Melinda's neck with his right hand. He pulled her towards himself by the neck.

"Now, you die," he whispered, then kissed her on the lips. Krishna kicked the wheelchair out of the way and pushed Melinda to the floor. The old woman was flapping in fear. Krishna turned her onto her stomach. He put the sickle under her neck and stomped on the back of her neck till the head came off. The boot saved him from injuring his leg in the process. After he was done, Krishna put the heads back in his bag.

***

After editing the video, Krishna left his PC as it started the rendering. He walked through a small door at the back of his studio, which led to a room with a big pigeonhole cabinet-sized 20x20. Twenty holes of the cabinet were filled with one head each. Krishna placed Melinda's head in the hole named Srilekha and the constable's head in the adjacent one. Then, he took a long look at the heads of his grandmother, mother, and sister before leaving the room.

7

GARBAGE

by Hari Pudipeddi

Srinu blew the whistle and stopped in front of an old, brown building. It was six in the morning and he was starting off on his morning run of garbage collection. As usual, he went to the backyard and took the lid off a tall plastic container. Inside, there was a black garbage bag twisted into a knot at the top. He pulled it out and put it over his shoulder. As he walked back through the narrow alley, he peeped in through one of the open windows – it was dark and empty.

Ghosts must inhabit this place, he thought, for he saw no human traces in this house, but the trash bin was always full. Today, the bag was unusually heavy; it was weighing him down, so he quickly hurried out and dumped the bag in the box-shaped blue cart and pedalled ahead.

Three months ago, Srinu had turned sixteen and had been about to enter college, when Murthy, his father, who worked two jobs as a security guard for Alwal High School in the morning and an ATM at night had disappeared one day without a trace. Srinu's life had taken a disastrous fall after that.

There was no way his mother could have managed the fees for his college, so he dropped out of Engineering and started working as a Garbage Collector for the GHMC in the cantonment. Ravi Mama, his maternal uncle, and a clerk in the Alwal Municipal office, had gotten him the job.

He still wished every day for his father to return home. But it was turning into a far-fetched dream with each passing day.

At around 1:30 p.m., with his morning round completed, Srinu cycled towards the dumping yard. When he entered through the creaking gate, there was already a ten-foot-high pile of garbage.

He parked behind the pile and started emptying the cart into a smaller one. Usually, the other boys scanned and sifted the garbage to retrieve any items of value – from damaged mobiles to liquor bottles to newspapers. But Srinu would simply dump everything he had collected and would head home.

That wasn't to be the case today.

As he reached for the last garbage bag in the cart – the one from the brown building, he struggled to lift it out and it fell to the ground. The knot loosened and the trash spilled out. Srinu approached the fallen cover and gasped in horror at the contents that fell out.

Srinu's heart pounded like the passing train behind him as he looked at the two-thousand-rupee notes sprawled on the ground. After several moments of silence, he scrambled to pick them up. He counted twenty notes.

Forty thousand.

Speechless, he stared blankly for a few moments before reaching for the garbage bag to stuff the notes back in. Looking inside, he inhaled sharply – inside were more notes in bundles. Sweating, he slipped in a trembling hand into the bag, as far as his arm could go.

He scanned his surroundings and found the yard deserted. Nobody had seen him or the money. Sneakily, Srinu put the bag back in the cart and rode out.

***

Three masked men attacked Murthy at 2:30 a.m. While he lay bleeding from his head, they broke the two ATMs and emptied the bundles of cash into gunny bags. As they were leaving, Murthy managed to trip the last of the masked men to the floor. There they lay, struggling, Murthy trying to peel the mask off his face – and he did succeed but right then a foot pinned his arm to the floor while a boot made contact with his jaw.

Murthy passed out, looking at the blurry face which seemed eerily familiar.

The ATM had been loaded with cash only the previous morning. The robbers got away with twenty-five lakhs. The police recorded Murthy's statement after he regained consciousness in the hospital and were investigating the robbery but had no leads. The security cameras installed inside the ATM had been disabled.

But Murthy was troubled by something else – the face he saw. He failed to conjure up the image in his mind. The head injury and the sedatives that kept him drowsy didn't help either. Three days later, when he was discharged and sent home, he was still lost in thought about the face.

'I know that face', he told himself, 'If only I could recollect it.'

Another two days passed. While watching an advertisement on the local cable channel, Murthy sprang up to his feet. The face returned to him. It was on TV.

Despite his headache, Murthy grabbed a shirt. "I'll need to inform the police," he mumbled under his breath as he walked out onto the street.

That was the last he was seen.

After searching for a week, the police concluded the case, saying, "Maybe he was in on it all along."

***

Srinu hadn't believed them then, nor did he even now. Going to the police with the money would only worsen the situation, he decided. So, he rode past the police station with his head bowed and directly went home.

The front door stood wide open and he could hear the sound of the TV. His mother was usually back home from work by this time, but the one-room house seemed deserted.

Maybe she's in the bathroom, he thought, but then, why is the front door open?

The weight of the garbage bag over his shoulder and the money inside didn't allow him to think further. He quickly bolted the door, sat down on the floor, and started pulling out the bundles of cash.

Even after stacking twenty bundles, the bag was only half-empty. He continued to pull out more bundles and added them to the stack. A few minutes later, as he reached deeper inside, Srinu felt something wet on his fingers. Looking at the topmost note, Srinu dropped the bundle to the floor.

There were bloodstains on it.

He found himself reaching into the bag again, and the next four bundles he brought out were drenched in red. He dropped them all, aside from the clean stack.

Putting his hand inside again, Srinu's fingers grazed something soft and round. As he felt around, tapping, he thought he was touching an ear. He immediately pulled out his hand – and found a blood-soaked note stuck to his fingers.

He lashed his hand. The note flew and stuck to the TV screen.

He knew what was inside, but he was in utter denial. His attempt to shut off his mind failed, so he flung the garbage bag across the room. It rolled under the TV table, the cover wrapping around the object inside.

He shuddered, staring at it.

Finally, holding his breath, and ignoring the silent screams in his head, Srinu reached for the garbage bag. He unwrapped the cover and put a trembling hand inside. His chest burned as his fingers wrapped around a tuft of hair. Slowly, he pulled it out, dreading and knowing what it would be.

And whose it would be.

When he stared into his father's dead eyes, Srinu fell to his knees. He used his left hand to catch hold of the head from dropping to the floor. Now, with his father's head held between both his hands, Srinu couldn't hold his tears anymore.

He screamed at the top of his lungs.

Two things happened in quick succession. First, he heard the name 'Murthy' from the TV and looked up. The note dripped off the screen and fell to the floor, leaving a blood trail.

A police officer was speaking, "Worked as a Security Guard in the ATM. We suspected him concerning the robbery earlier. This morning, at around 5:30 a.m., we received a call from an unknown number. It was him. He told us that he was being held captive in an old, abandoned house. By the time we reached there—"

The screen now cut to the old brown building. A background voice said, "The police reached here around 6:30 a.m., following Murthy's call, to a bloodbath, we are being told. They found three dead bodies in the cellar, out of which, police have positively identified one as that of Ravi's, one of the three robbers."

Ravi Mama. Srinu's body went cold.

The host now asked a question and the reporter answered, "… one of the dead bodies is beheaded, we hear, and the head is missing."

Right then, there was a heavy knock at the door. Before he could react, the door was broken down and in walked a heavy-built man. On the TV, Srinu heard about the third robber, "…who is currently missing, is a local gym owner, Suresh…"

The screen cut to the advertisement of a gym named Booming Body. Srinu turned from the TV to the man in the room.

Ravi Mama's friend, Suresh, was smiling at him.

***

"We were going to let him go, but your Mama got emotional. Your father acted smart and stole his phone. And so, we had to kill him."

Srinu's grip tightened on his father's head. He slowly moved it to his chest to calm himself down, but the tears wouldn't stop.

"Ravi turned out to be a thorn after that, so I put him to rest as well. And then, I saw my chance to have all the money for myself." He pointed to the TV and smiled again.

"Why?" Srinu's voice broke.

"I had to find a safe passage for the money. Then I thought of you. I decided to give you a gift for the help – one final look at your father."

Suresh laughed, and rage started building up inside Srinu. He threw Murthy's head at Suresh's face and scrambled across the room to the kitchen corner. He picked up a grinding stone and slammed it on the gym trainer's leg. Suresh's left foot was crushed, and he jerked back, yelping in pain.

Limping, he picked up the gas cylinder off the ground with a single hand and stepped towards Srinu. He kicked Murthy's head out of the way. Seeing this, Srinu went berserk. He frantically looked around for something.

His eyes fell on the *Boti* – a knife cut into a wooden platform. He ducked and reached for it, while Suresh screamed and crashed the cylinder into the wall behind him.

Srinu was in a corner now, holding the *Boti* in his raised arms as Suresh approached him. Just then, there was a loud scream, followed by a wooden chair breaking against Suresh's head. A woman hurried to his side and sat down next to him as Suresh writhed in pain, trying to make sense of what happened.

Srinu started crying the moment he saw her. "I'm here now, don't worry," she consoled him. He let go of the *Boti* and calmed down a little. His mother looked up into Suresh's eyes as they met hers. She blinked and her mouth curved to the right, giving a subtle half-smile.

It's this innocent and beguiling smile that brought me this far, Suresh thought, but couldn't stop himself from smiling.

Srinu didn't notice the knife his mother pulled from behind her back.

8

YOU HAVE A NOTIFICATION

by Akhilesh M.

The phone buzzed with a message, which read, "I'm sick, I need help. It's urgent. PLEASE!" He ignored it. After all, it was she who had moved away, saying that she didn't need him anymore. A part of him longed to reply her text. But he didn't.

He got down from the bed and out to the balcony, inhaling the breeze brushing against his face at 2 a.m. in the night. The dogs were on their night orchestra, and the swing was screeching in the garden while the clouds were playing hide-and-seek with the moon and stars.

Soon, his thoughts travelled to the past, reminiscing – how he had met her, how she had tried to impress him, how they got along with each other, those silly fights, and those beautiful moments.

"Black or white?" she asked.

"Both," he replied with a smile.

"Excuse me?" She raised her eyebrows.

"I mean, I'll go with white."

"Well, fine," she nodded her head. The game started.

"Knight? Seriously?" She whispered, looking down. He smiled.

"Sorry! That was not a nice move!" She winked. He smiled again.

"Man! You're a silent killer!" She exclaimed. He smiled, yet again.

"Would you mind me killing your Queen?" she whispered.

"No, not at all!"

"Is it? Part of a strategy, I guess," she smiled.

"Maybe," he replied.

"And, that's a checkmate!" She beamed, adjusting her spectacles.

"That's not the end, dear! Here, try this!" He puffed air from the corner of his lips to his hair.

"Oops! I lost! Congratulations!" she mumbled sarcastically. He smiled ear-to-ear.

"What? At least say thank you! Why do you smile so much?" She questioned.

"I lost!" He replied.

"What?"

"Of all the black and white combinations I've ever seen, your eyes are the best. And I'm lost in them." He chuckled. With the chessboard aside, he witnessed a perfect checkmate.

Just then, his phone buzzed again. It was her. "PLEASE!" the text read. His gut told him something awful was going on. He sprinted down the stairs, not bothering to switch on the lights. He drove to her house at a dangerous speed.

As he reached, he called her, but there was no answer. It was dark as hell. Although he couldn't see, he could hear voices from inside. The main door was already unlocked, adding to his fear. He paused for a while and concentrated on her voice, which was the only way she could be reached. At last, he reached her bedroom. The voices grew louder as he approached. He shouted her name out loud and banged on the door.

He tried twisting the doorknob and it opened, but he couldn't see her. He passed his hand across the wall and tried to switch on the lights. There were none. He shouted her name aloud, yet again. This time, he heard her saying, "Here! On your right! Save me, please!" He turned right and moved forward. Despite anxiety numbing his bones, he mustered up the courage to take a few more steps forward.

"I'm in this room, please, please save me!" She cried.

He searched frantically for her. Suddenly, somebody kicked him from behind and he fell on the bed with a thud. As he turned around to take a look at the predator, his sight went hazy. He cleared his eyes and focused on the silhouette near the door. It took him a while to realise at whom he was staring, and the realisation made his insides scream with terror.

He was staring at his own self. Or perhaps, his doppelganger. The stranger had a grin on his face and seemed a bit muscular; a better version of himself. He couldn't believe his eyes. His face grew pale, and he could hear his own heart beating hard. She held the stranger's arm, and said, "Look! He was the one who tried to kill me! I'm so glad that you came!"

He couldn't understand a thing. *Is she thinking I'm him? Do I even look like myself?* He wondered and looked into the nearby mirror. The face staring back at him was not his. He had someone else's face. What on Earth was happening?

He shouted at her, "No! The person standing next to you is not me! I don't know who he is!" She passed her hands over the stranger's shoulder and whispered, "Finish him!" The stranger clenched the knife and came closer to him, but instead, turned around and stabbed her, right in the heart. She screamed and shrieked till her voice started to die down, and then she repeated over and over again, "I trusted you."

He knew she was actually referring to his original self. The stranger was his look-alike. As he tried to fight back, the stranger stabbed him in the abdomen. He felt weak as he slowly started losing the strength in his legs.

There he was, numb, leaning against a wall, amidst a pool of blood. He looked at her still body. Her eyes were open and bore a glassy look with all the colour drained from them.

He could feel the blood dripping down his abdomen. The stranger hovered over him in dominion.

"Who's he? Who's this monster?" He shouted as he turned unconscious.

"Hey! What happened? Relax! Maybe you had a bad dream," came a familiar voice from behind.

He cleared his eyes, gasping. There she was beside him, trying to cool him down.

"Nothing, just a nightmare," he sighed.

She whispered, "Hey, it's okay. I'm here."

He tried to go back to sleep again, gazing at her, thinking, the worst nightmare would be losing you.

***

My mom shouts from downstairs as I'm about to read the next chapter, "Akhil! It's already late. Shut the lights off and go to bed!"

"Fine, maa!" I reply.

It's just the second chapter of the novel, and I'm really into it. I must thank my friend for the recommendation. I go into the balcony and feel the cool breeze. The swing is screeching in the garden. A few moments later, I make my bed and am about to drift off to sleep.

Abruptly, my phone buzzes. The air is sucked out of my lungs as I read, "I'm sick, I need help. It's urgent. Please!"

9

THE HAUNTED BUNGALOW

by Salbaz Sayyed

It was 2019. My company had issued my transfer to Goa and had even offered me a bungalow. Once we were all settled, my wife Maya and I lay on the mattresses we'd put in the hall for the time being. Since we were both exhausted, we agreed to grab dinner in a restaurant. It was past 11:00 p.m. when we returned, and my son Nikhil had already fallen asleep in my arms.

We opened the door and it creaked. "Isn't this house new?" Maya asked, puzzled. "Well, my boss said it was renovated a month ago," I shrugged, equally confused. As good as new, he'd said to me while signing the papers.

"Then why is the door creaking? It sounds like it has caught rust."

"I'm sure it must be the coldness of the winter, Jaan. Don't worry."

"Uh-oh, looks like we left Nikhil's bedroom light on," she said, squinting her eyes at me, "You can't do a thing properly, can you?" *Oops,* I thought sheepishly. *That was weird, though. I remembered having turned them off.*

Maya's eyes widened in panic. "Do you think someone broke in?"

"You're always so paranoid, Maya," I shake my head and put my jacket on the bed. "Let's go to bed, it's late."

The next morning, as I was leaving for work, Nikhil and Maya were figuring out where to put the rest of the stuff. While Maya dusted every item she took out from the box, she watched Nikhil talking to himself in a corner. Amused, she asked him who it was. "Maa, this is Akshay. May I play ball with him?" he asked, and Maya laughed. "Sure, darling. Sharing is caring. Hi, Akshay," she said, humouring him. Nikhil continued to mumble as Maya headed to the kitchen. *Kids,* she thought chuckled.

The moment I came home, Nikhil ran towards me. "Papa!" he shouted joyfully and jumped in my arms. I held him and ruffled his hair. "What did my *beta* do today?" I asked, putting down my bag.

"I made a new friend, Papa. His name is Akshay."

"Wow, that's good. Does he stay close by?"

"No, papa. He lives in my room."

I laughed. "Could he stay with us?" he asked, and I nodded, still laughing.

"Ravi?" Maya called out. I turned to her, and my grin faded after seeing her grim expression. That night, we were all in bed when I heard a blood-curdling scream from Nikhil's room. Maya panicked and grabbed my hand. "What was that?" she squeaked. We ran towards Nikhil's room to find him crying. "What's wrong?" I asked, looking at Nikhil's moist eyes.

"Akshay hit me and stole my toy," he wailed.

This nonsense was getting too much to bear. I lost my cool. "Nikhil, stop this nonsense. Your imaginary friend cannot steal your toy. Go back to sleep now."

Maya looked at me nervously and hurried to his bedside. I stormed off to the kitchen to get a glass of water. "Go to sleep, Nikhil. Look, if you want, I'll punish Akshay for misbehaving with you," I overheard them talking from the kitchen, "But mummy, he is not standing there. Look, he is on the other side."

Entering Nikhil's room, I found Maya sitting there, frozen in shock, her eyes staring unblinkingly into the void. "Maya," I called out, and she jerked up. "What happened?" "Hmm? Nothing. I'm just tucking him in."

Back in our room, Maya snuggled close to me, burying her head in my chest. "Ravi, I think I saw a dark figure in Nikhil's room." I scoffed. "Don't be silly, Maya. Are you hallucinating, too? Nikhil is a child, and he hasn't made any friends here. He's probably just lonely."

"I guess you're right, but I'm worried, Ravi. This house feels strange."

"Don't worry. It's a new environment. With time, we'll feel at home."

Morning peaked in through the curtains, and all three of us overslept. "Nikhil! Nikhil! Wake up. You'll be late for school. It is 8 o'clock already," I heard Maya call out as I poured two cups of tea for the both of us.

As I gazed outside the window, I couldn't help but marvel at the view. As my eyes fixated on the greenery adding to the vista, the tranquillity of the morning was disrupted by a shrill, ear-piercing shriek. My heart thundering against my chest, I sprinted to Nikhil's room.

My breath caught up in my throat at the sight in front of me. Nikhil was in his car bed, badly wounded. "Look at our son!"

Maya cried hysterically, falling to the ground. Blood was dripping off both his elbows and there was a huge cut on his forehead.

I couldn't bear to see it. My baby boy was lying there, unconscious, unmoving. As I moved closer to him, his eyes fluttered open momentarily. What I saw made me take several steps back. His eyeballs were swollen, big, and dark. A few seconds later, he collapsed again.

Without a second thought, we rushed him to the hospital. My wife couldn't stop weeping and I was trembling to the depths of my bones. *Nothing is wrong with my boy*, I kept assuring myself. They took him to the ER. Even after an hour, the doctors rushed past us without any explanation.

Finally, a doctor gestured to us to see him outside, his expression grave. "Unfortunately, it was too late, Mr. Ravi." I felt the blood drain off my face. "We tried our best to save him." He continued, "I am so sorry for your loss." I couldn't utter a word. Maya shrieked and cried hysterically.

"There was something else, Mr. Ravi," the doctor added. "It's a very unusual thing, but when we ran a couple of tests, we found some traces of skin under his nail – traces of rotten flesh."

I was startled. Maya looked as though she would faint any minute. "What does that mean, doctor?" She managed to speak. "We can only know the details after getting the post-mortem report," he concluded. Maya couldn't stop sobbing. "I'd like to see our son," I said finally. After spending an entire day at the hospital, we reached home late in the evening. Maya and I were too grief-stricken to talk. What was my boy's fault? He was such an innocent soul.

The funeral was a day later. Ours was a small family, so not many had gathered to say their final goodbyes. That entire day, Maya and I barely spoke. We were still hoping for all this to be an ugly nightmare. But we couldn't hide from the truth. Nikhil, my little boy, my only child, was no more. I wanted to get home and get to the root of it all. How could my son be attacked this badly right inside the house? "We will figure this out, Maya," I said to her as I parked my car in the driveway.

But when we opened the door, what we saw shocked us even more. All the boxes, dishes, clothes, were in the air. I could not believe my eyes. The moment we stepped in, everything rained down on us.

The dishes broke, the boxes scattered, and it all piled into a big mess. "Oh my god! What is happening to our house?" Maya yelled. "I have no idea," I shouted back and turned towards her. I was still trying to fathom everything happening that day when we heard a loud thud.

I stepped out to see the TV fallen to the ground. I moved closer, and the TV fell back to the side. The screen went blank for a few seconds, then suddenly lit up with the face of a little boy all bruised and wounded, saying, "You hurt me. It's time to pay."

He growled and hissed inhumanely, and I jumped back with a jerk. The TV turned on and off a few times before blinking into a red screen. Then I felt something grab my collar and pull me across the living room. I tried to shout, but my voice was stuck in my throat. I was thrown against the window and my head banged against the iron grill. I writhed in pain before everything became still.

***

"Baba, Baba... Baba," I heard someone call me. *"Yo munis uthana kitak?* (Why isn't this man waking up?)" A man muttered in Konkani.

I slowly opened my eyes. It was our neighbour, Peter. It took a few moments for me to recollect what happened. *"Devak argaa, yo jivit asa.* (Thank god, he's alive.)"

"Where am I?" I asked.

"In your house," Peter said, puzzled. "We heard screams and got worried. We darted here as fast as we could." Suddenly, I remembered. "Maya! Where is she?" I asked, panicking.

"Calm down, she's inside. My wife is talking to her," Peter said. "I should've warned you the day you came. I am so sorry you lost your son."

"Warned me about what?"

Peter sighed. "In 2010, a couple had bought this bungalow from a rich fish merchant from Goa. In a couple of years, they were blessed with a baby boy. But the father was a drunkard and a gambler. He would come home every night and abuse both the wife and the son.

"One night, he was more drunk than usual and murdered his son with a screwdriver because he stole a child's dinosaur toy. The wife couldn't take the trauma and stabbed herself too. Ever since then, their spirits have haunted the house. It is that little boy's soul that killed your son. And now the lady's spirit wants your blood."

I felt sick. I was never a man who believed in ghosts and spirits but what was happening in front of my eyes was unexplainable. I went in. Maya was talking to Peter's wife. She had tears in her eyes and looked miserable. "You must leave this house at once. It is not healthy for you or Ravi," she said, and Maya nodded. I knew what I had to do.

***

2 Years Later

"Nikhil, come beta," Maya beamed proudly at our 1-year-old son as he took his first step. Adopting a child was the best decision I ever made. Maya and I had to find a way to cope with our loss. Our bungalow was cleansed after the pandit performed the last rites on Akshay's and his mother's soul.

My wife and I started a charity home for children who were victims of mental trauma, abuse, or exploitation. All we hoped to do was to make sure that there wouldn't be another Akshay or Nikhil who would lose their innocent lives to murders committed by wicked people on earth.

10

THE CASE

by Prajwal Shukla

There he was – lying on my couch, staring at the wall and squinting his eyes, his head tilted to the side. I decided it was better to let him be. Every day was getting weirder; every hour was a mindless routine of persistent sitting. Every minute of this pathetic state Brij was in made me nauseous.

I kept trying to search for a distraction to take his mind off his agony, but there were some things you couldn't control. I made him some *chai*, which he accepted absent-mindedly. I tried striking up a conversation, but he chose silence over small talk. The neighbours were in for a silent treat that day, contrary to the banter they usually got to hear. Just then, the doorbell rang.

I answered it only to find Hope there, with a case for him. I couldn't have been more grateful to her for finally bringing along a distraction. This should be good, I thought. I took Hope to Brij to inform him about the case. This was the first time I saw him relax after ages. "Oh, sweet Hope, always to the rescue," Brij said welcomingly. Happily, I saw him take the first sip of his tea, which he spat right out.

"It's cold. Make me another one while I tend to Hope. And please hurry up, will you? We've got a case to solve."

"Right," I murmured, as I turned the flame back on again.

"Here you go," I said, bringing him his second cup a while later.

"You forgot two sugars," he said, and then remarked, "Your stirring is slow, and you didn't turn the stove to a low flame before straining the tea."

"Just drink the damn *chai.*"

Ignoring our argument, Hope began, "This one is complicated. We received a complaint at midnight. A resident in a housing society found blood in the tap water. On investigating, we found a body floating in the water tank belonging to Mr. Mehta, a resident, 48. We assumed the blood was his."

"Do you have the forensics report?" I asked.

"We wanted Brij to check the scene first," said Hope. "The body and blood samples are already being examined."

"And apparently," added Brij, "There have been complaints about multiple persons missing from the same society."

"How did you –" I gaped at him, then realisation dawned. "How long have you been tailing them?"

"I was upset, not stupid." That sounded like the Brij I first met.

We went to the scene. Handing me the missing persons' report, Hope went on to show Brij the rest of it.

"Where did you say the wound was again?" asked Brij.

"There wasn't any."

Brij's eyes twinkled. "No wound and lots of blood. Things just got interesting." He grinned. After carefully re-examining the scene for Brij's benefit, there was nothing left to do but wait for the forensic report to arrive.

A few hours later, the tension at home felt tense. Our breathing was heavy, and our eyes were focused on the chessboard. It was beginning to look like we were stuck in a stalemate. Just then, the doorbell rang.

Hope was here with the forensics report and some news. She looked disoriented and weary. Asking for a glass of water, she sat down and handed us the file. Brij slowly smiled which slowly turned into a grin.

"What's the matter?" I asked.

"They've found two DNA samples in the blood; one is Mr. Mehta's, and the other is unknown. There are traces of a weird substance on the victim, which they haven't been able to identify yet." He said. "Hope? Have they gathered DNA samples of the four missing people and cross-checked them, in case it belongs to one of them?"

"Yes, those reports will be brought in later today. What do you think this could be about?"

"Well, they had no direct connection in the society. But four people from the same age group going missing in the same week, and then a dead body with no known connection to them shows up. Plus, the murder weapon is still missing. This case is unravelling a bigger mystery than just a group of neighbours having an unfortunate coincidence."

"And what's that?"

"Do you mind adding more ginger to my *chai*? It's cold outside."

As I went back to make another cup, he began. "The day we were at the crime scene with Hope, there was a resident yelling at security because somebody had parked in his spot. After asking, the guard said that the car seemed to have been there for quite some time."

"But what's it to do with the case?" asked Hope.

"Out of the two DNA samples you've found, one of them has to be of the culprit's. What if it's not anyone from the missing suspects? The resident hadn't seen the car before, and residents have their own parking lots. So, we have an outsider. The car could be that person's and there's a possibility that he or she is still in the building."

"And our missing suspects?"

"They found themselves in an unfortunate situation and had to help with getting rid of the body."

Hope decided to head back and check this angle out. Brij asked her to find out if the traces of the substance found on the dead body could be anywhere the dead body had been a day before the time of death and to get an update on the car.

I was done with the tea by the time she left, which he sipped appreciatively.

"So these four people helped dispose of a body and went into hiding?" I asked.

"If you were an outsider with blood on your hands in a residential society, and you took help from four unfortunate bystanders to get rid of the body, where would you go?"

"So, you're saying that our victim knew the killer and they had a fight, which explains the second blood type. The killer found the four missing residents and they helped him dispose of the body, and then blood leaked from the body, along with the culprit's blood from the wound. And the five of them then hid in the building itself. But where?"

Half an hour passed by; Brij kept pacing back and forth the living room. He finally nestled on the couch and closed his eyes to think again, and within five minutes, sprang back victoriously.

"The construction site in the basement!"

"I'm sorry, the what?"

"There's always been a major pipeline leakage, abandoned today, but passing under the building. It leads out to the river 60 kilometres south from there but there are other service spots on the way where they could've easily gotten off and walked away. The missing four are probably hiding at our killer's place now. If our killer and the victim briefly knew each other, let's assume the killer also knew where Mehta lived. The outsider must have dropped his keys in the apartment and could have gone there to look for them and ended up finding the blueprints of the building that he had. The victim was an authorised and elected representative of the building and was taking responsibility for the pipeline fixtures. That's where they got their escapade. But he has to come back for the car, today or tomorrow. That's when we get him and the rest of them."

"What about the substance on Mehta?"

Brij's face turned grim. "I have reason to believe it was the same substance they found on her."

"Is that what this is all about? Her? It's always been her, hasn't it?" It was all coming back to the incident that had left him rattled. "She was just, just there Brij. It was an accident. What do you think? That someone put the same substance in her? And that's why she jumped?"

"I always suspected that, Chatur," said Brij. "I was just waiting for a case like this. Now I can find the substance, find out what it does, find where it comes from, find who makes it, and avenge Binny's death."

Just then, the doorbell rang again. I opened the door and was surprised to find Hope. She walked into the room, a small smile playing on her lips. "Looks like you were right," she said.

"Right about what?" I asked.

"The car in the parking belongs to Rick Gonzales and the second DNA we found also matches his."

"Who's Rick Gonzales?"

"A local supplier working for a massive drug organization. He appears to be a rookie minding his own business; never killed anyone before. We had two officers secretly watching the place, waiting for him, and finally caught Gonzales as he tried to sneak his car out of the building. Following him to the place where all the missing residents were hiding, we brought them to the station for interrogation."

"Great. My work here is done," said Brij.

There was something off about him. I wondered if he was still thinking about her. His wife, Binny, had seemingly dropped down from a twenty-four-storey building while at a college reunion. The reports showed a substance in her bloodstream, but nothing from the records matched with it. They couldn't identify what the compound was and due to lack of evidence, they couldn't arrest anyone. Brij had known since day one that something had been done to her. Ever since then, he waited for another case to show up with similarities.

"Brij, what's the matter?" I asked softly. He was staring at Hope as if wanting to say something. "You were in charge of this case as well as Binny's. It was you who convinced me that they didn't identify the substance. I didn't see the report." His voice was a steely whisper.

"Brij –"

"You know, don't you? You have known all this time." His voice was rising.

"Look, I –" Something flashed in Hope's eyes. Guilt?

"You know!" Brij yelled. "You have always known!"

"This is for your own good!" Hope broke down. "It's a new drug, synthetic, but its origins are natural, somehow. It's been widely used as a psychedelic. Wherever Binny's reunion was, they must have done drugs, and Binny must have been part of the pack. It's a secret, a hidden demon of the cartel world that was summoned back to life by a scientific research team. They were trying to replicate the whole genome of psychedelic plants that died out in history as an experiment. They didn't expect it to turn out this way. Nobody did. We have a feeling that the organization with which Rick works plays a huge role in the workings of this cartel. These are really dangerous people, Brij. Hunting them down by yourself is stupidity."

"What's it called?"

"I can't tell you. It's a government secret."

"Fine. I'll search for it myself."

"You can't!" Hope snapped. "Do you hear me? It's too dangerous. Even a great mind like yours can't get out of the web of death once they seek you out. And it'll be a piece of cake for them."

"Let me help you. Please. You know you will need it. I just want justice for Binny. Nobody will know it was you. Your reputation as a cop will not be harmed in any way. Just tell me what it is."

Hope sighed in defeat, rubbed her hands on her face, and looked Brij in the eye. "The Magician's Cape."

11

LOVE, FRIENDSHIP AND MURDER PART I

by Sameem Hassain

*T*his is going to be awesome, buddy," I hooted, "Pass me another pint." I was driving the car single-handedly with a beer bottle in my other, much to David's dismay.

"Kabir, that's enough! You've already had enough booze," he scolded, pulling the bottle away.

"Come on, we're not kids anymore," I replied, pouting at him.

"Kabir, stop the car! You're drunk. It's not safe if you drive further."

"Where is Taaha? Did she reach home from the party?" I asked, ignoring his warning.

"Yes, she did. For god's sake, stop the car, Kabir. You're going at 150 km per hour."

I increased the volume of the stereo.

"Stop the car, please!" David pleaded with me.

"Give me the pint, David."

"No!"

"Give it to me," I whined.

"Watch out!" David screamed.

We heard a thud as the car went over a huge bump. Shit. I had run someone over.

I jolted upright, took deep breaths, and looked around. It was the same recurring nightmare. Muttering curses under my breath, I turned towards Neha sleeping beside me, hoping I hadn't woken her up.

Something seemed off. I switched on the bedside lamp for a clearer view and my heart stopped beating. Everything around me came crashing down as I stared at Neha's blood-spattered body with a knife stabbed in her stomach.

***

"So, Mr. Kabir, I'm asking you once again: why should we believe you had nothing to do with your wife's murder?" the inspector questioned.

"Sir, why will I kill the only person in my life? I loved her so much. She didn't deserve to die," I wept.

It was true. We were extremely happy, and now, everything had gone down in a flash. Neha had been murdered in cold blood. The police arrived within minutes and people gathered all around. To make matters worse, I was being held under suspicion.

"Confess now, when you can. Or else, it won't take long before the tables turn on you," the inspector said.

"Sir, she meant everything to me."

"Maybe you found out she was cheating on you?"

"She had such a pure soul. She not only helped me battle depression, but also prevented me from committing suicide – twice. Her love healed me and gave me a renewed sense of hope," I said, gaping at him in disbelief.

"I read your name in an accident case a year ago," he mentioned.

I turned quiet. Guilt started to rise. Poor David.

"Speak up."

"That's enough, sir. You can't accuse him without concrete evidence," said a voice. Taaha walked in through the door along with a lawyer. He gazed angrily at Taaha.

"Let him go. Show us evidence and then drag him into custody," she reprimanded.

***

"What if I give birth to a boy?" Neha asked, staring into my eyes. We were lazing on our bed, cuddling.

"I want a girl, my love," I kissed her forehead.

"Nope, boy it is," she argued.

"Okay! We'll have both," I laughed, kissing her lovingly.

"Kabir?"

I was snatched back to reality. Taaha sat opposite me in a random coffee shop. Why would somebody kill Neha? Tears started to spill, and I broke down, holding Taaha's hands.

"Eat something, Kabir."

"I am not worth living, Taaha. God is punishing me for my sins."

"Don't say that, Kabir. You're being punished for nothing. I have to leave now, but I'll be back by evening."

"Okay, thank you," I managed to say.

Taaha, David, and I had been friends since college. We used to enjoy a lot, but ever since then, things had changed. Stumbling out of the café, I walked straight into the nearest bar and ordered a whiskey neat.

"Keep 'em coming," I grumbled to the bartender. Every mistake I'd made in my life began to roll in front of me like a slideshow on loop. I drank till I passed out.

***

"Kabir, wake up! The inspector called and wants to meet you." Taaha's voice pierced through the phone into my hazy senses before the call ended. I opened my eyes groggily and looked around. I was in a hotel bed. A good shower later, I was seated opposite the officer, my anxiety doing somersaults.

"Do you know how she was murdered?" the inspector asked.

"Multiple stabs and a knife in her stomach, sir," I muttered, a question rather than a statement.

The inspector took a deep breath. "No, Kabir. The autopsy reports are here. Neha was poisoned. The poison was injected into her bloodstream five to six hours before she died; the report shows the time of death to be around 1:00 am," he said. The hair on my neck started to rise, my mind in a whirlwind of emotions.

"So she must have been poisoned between 7 p.m. and 8 p.m. I remember she wasn't home till 9:30 p.m. that day, so she was poisoned before that," I said softly, trying to focus.

"Absolutely. We cross-checked with your office staff. They informed us that you were at work during that time. You couldn't have done it," he said. I refrained from rolling my eyes at him for stating the obvious. "Did you talk to Neha's office staff?" I asked instead.

He nodded. "According to the staff biometric, she left the office at 8:30 pm."

"Then what about the stabs?" I managed to ask.

"Our theory is that the killer wasn't satisfied with poisoning her, so they broke into your house and stabbed her relentlessly till they were," he said.

I was unable to breathe. What kind of monster could do this?

"Weirdly enough, you didn't even stir during the whole thing," the inspector said with a hint of suspicion.

Guilt gripped me again. It had been David's birthday that night. I had driven myself to drunkenness to ease the pain I had to live with. "I'm sorry. I'd had too much to drink. I didn't even notice Neha coming home. I was already fast asleep."

"Do you suspect anyone who would have wanted to harm her?" He asked.

"As per my knowledge, there were two people who disturbed her," I said.

"Who are they?"

"Hari and Gopal."

He looked at me expectantly, urging me to go on.

"Hari was her ex-boyfriend, and Gopal is her colleague. Hari used to torture her in the past after their break-up. Gopal used to flirt with her in office. It made her uneasy, but she never filed a serious complaint."

"Let's speak with Gopal first," decided the inspector.

***

"How can I help you?" the receptionist peered at us over her monitor.

"We're here to see Mr. Gopal," said the inspector in an authoritative tone.

"Please wait there." She gestured to the waiting room, intimidated by Mr. Das. Ten minutes later, a tall, muscular man stood in front of us. "Yes, I'm Gopal. What do you want?" he asked, the tone of irritation too noticeable in his question.

"Come to the station, Gopal. Let's discuss what we want," said Mr. Das.

In a split second, he pushed Mr. Das and ran out of there. Mr. Das and I sprinted after him. Gopal looked over his shoulder as he kept on running. Mr. Das sped up.

"Don't try to run, we know you killed Neha," Mr. Das bellowed.

Gopal stopped running. Mr. Das punched him hard and held him tightly by the collar. "Tell me, why did you kill her? What did she do?" I asked angrily.

"Hold on. Is Neha dead?" he asked in genuine confusion.

"Don't act smart, Gopal," Mr. Das seethed.

"Why would I hurt her? I liked her. I asked her to join me for coffee twice or thrice, that's it."

"Then why did you run from us?" Mr. Das asked, sceptical.

"I thought you people came for…" He trailed off.

"Came for?" Mr. Das questioned furiously.

"Marijuana," he muttered. Mr. Das slapped him, harder this time. After a couple of minutes, my phone rang.

"Who is this?" I asked.

"Sir, I'm Nair, your apartment watchman."

"Nair, I am busy right now, can I talk to you later?"

"Sir, it's about Neha Ji."

I stepped aside from Mr. Das. "What is it?" I asked uncertainly.

"I can't tell you that over a phone call. Can we meet?" He pleaded.

"I'll be there," I said, hanging up.

***

"Tell me, Nair, what is it?" Half an hour later, I was back home, panting more out of fear than from being out of breath.

"Sir, actually…" he struggled to speak.

"Nair, you can tell me," I said, holding his shoulders, looking into his eyes.

"Sir, I saw Mehta Ji speaking with someone that night. I think it might've been Neha madam."

"You mean Mehta from 401?" I asked.

"Yes, sir. He looked suspicious to me. He even held her hand and tried to tell her something. At the same time, there was a power cut in our street, so I didn't have a clear vision."

"Then, what happened next?" I asked, impatient.

"I don't know, sir. I came back to work."

"Is he at home now?"

"His wife and children went out of town exactly the day after Neha Ji's incident. He hasn't been seen since."

"Do you have his number?" I urged.

"Yes sir, here it is."

I tried calling his number, but it went to voicemail.

"Shit! It's not working. Anyway, thank you, Nair. Keep this 500 with you," I said, offering him money.

"No, sir. Neha madam was always so kind to me. She used to spend a lot of time with my kids. I hope the killer is caught soon, sir," he said. Despite the circumstances, I felt proud of Neha.

"Where can I find Mehta Ji?" I asked.

"I'll give you his wife's number, contact her." After a few rings, Mrs. Mehta answered. "Hello," she said.

"Yes, can I talk to Mehta Ji?" I asked.

"Who is this?"

"I'm Suresh, Mehta ji's colleague," I lied, "I couldn't reach him. I wanted to have a word with him."

"I'm at my native's, Suresh Ji. I'm a bit worried. He hasn't even called me since a few days. The last time this happened, he had partied too much with his colleagues and crashed god knows where."

"Don't worry, I'm sure he has just been busy with work. Do you have any idea where I could find him?"

"We have a guest house in the outskirts of the city," she said after a pause. "He occasionally used to go with his friends."

"Could you tell me the address, please? I'll go and check."

"I'll text you, Suresh Ji. Please check and let me know." She hung up.

It took forever to reach the guest house. Opening the gate of the creepy-looking bungalow, I treaded carefully, watching my step. I went to knock on the main door, but to my surprise, it was already ajar. I stepped in and was immediately hit with a stingy, unbearable odour. Amidst the darkness, I pulled out my phone from my pocket and switched the flashlight on.

That's when I saw the source of the smell. Disgust mixed with terror clutched my heart as I saw Mehta tied to a chair, unmoving, and stabbed multiple times in the stomach.

12

LOVE, FRIENDSHIP AND MURDER PART II

by Sameem Hassain

*D*avid wasn't in his seat. I staggered out from the car. We were enveloped by the darkest hour of the night. The car had hit a pole, incurring a lot of damage. David stood behind me, at a distance.

"David!" I screamed.

That's when I noticed someone lying on the road. I ran towards him. It was an old man in his 70's.

"Oh my god! What have I done?" Fear seeped in as I tried to make sense of things, "We killed this man. We killed this poor old man."

"Kabir," David said almost inaudibly, "nothing is going to happen. I'll call the police and explain everything."

"What do you mean?"

"I begged you to drive slowly," he chastised, "Now, look at me. Nothing is going to happen. I'm calling them. Not a word out of you," he warned, gripping my shoulders.

It wasn't long before the police arrived. David gestured to me to stay away. I stood on the footpath, watching them speak. Suddenly, they started hauling David towards the jeep. Panicking, I rushed to the officer.

"Sir, what happened? Why is he being taken?" I asked.

"He confessed that he drove over that old man. He'll be going in for a long time," said the officer. I was about to tell him the truth but stopped when I saw David signalling me to keep quiet with his eyes. We were both taken to the police station.

"Why are you doing this?" I hissed under my breath.

"You once saved me in an accident years ago, remember?"

"That was ages ago! How is this related to that?" I almost shouted, impatient.

"I never got a chance to repay you," he smiled sadly.

"Are you crazy? You'll be in jail for years," my voice choked as tears pricked my eyes.

"Don't forget me, brother. I'll come back soon." He winked light-heartedly.

"Kabir?"

I jolted up. "Yes Das Ji," I said, wiping my tears.

"The autopsy reports have come. Apart from the stab wounds on Mehta's body, there was no poison found in his body, and no clues or fingerprints were left at the crime scene."

"What about his relatives, friends, and wife? Can we talk to them?" I asked.

"No luck. I cross-checked everything. He had quite a good reputation in the society and with his family."

"I think somehow Mehta's murder is linked with Neha's."

"Maybe. We are back to square one," he sighed exasperatedly.

"Das Ji, let's talk to Hari. Neha and Hari were in love for three years. He kept pestering her even after our marriage. I have a gut feeling that he might be our killer," I said.

***

"Can we talk to Hari?" I asked the receptionist.

"I'll intimate him. Please have a seat." She gestured for us to sit.

We were in his photo studio. Sneaking a glance at the pictures on the walls, I noticed they looked different. There was pain, suffering, affliction, torture, and agony lurking in them. After five minutes, he came out. "Hello, I'm Hari. How can I help you?" he said, extending his hand.

"We are here to talk about Neha," Mr. Das began. He looked bemused. He was manly, with wild, dark eyes and a rough long beard, portraying him even more so a killer.

"Can we sit and talk?" he requested. Upon agreement, he took us to the nearest café.

"Can we order? I need to drink something," he smiled. Signalling to the waiter, he said, "Two cappuccinos for these wonderful people over here."

"What about you, sir?" the waiter asked.

"Chai milegi?" ("May I get some tea?")

"Milegi, sir." ("Yes, sir.")

"You were asking me something?" He turned back to us after the waiter had left.

"Did you kill Neha?" I asked, brushing all etiquettes aside.

"Consider me honoured for the post," he grumbled.

"Don't play games with us. Tell us the truth," Mr. Das said through gritted teeth, his patience wearing thin.

All traces of humour were gone. "She was killed?" He stuttered.

"And you had motive," added Das ji.

"Why will I kill the only person I've ever loved in my entire life?" He choked, tears springing his eyes. I could see he was controlling himself.

Mr. Das and I shared a look.

"Come, let me show you something." He took us back to his studio.

We couldn't believe our eyes. The room in his studio was loaded with Neha's photos. Placing his hand on my shoulder, he began to speak, looking at them, "Do you know why I called her even after your marriage? I wanted her so badly. I begged her to come back, but she never responded. I cried till I could cry no more. Days passed, and I learnt to live with her memories instead of crying for her."

Sighing, I thanked him for his hospitality and decided to leave, disappointed at not having made any progress. What a pointless conversation, I thought, stepping out from his studio. I heard him call me and turned back.

"Can I tell you something?" He asked, catching up to me.

"Sure."

"There are types of killers. Some enjoy killing the person, while some enjoy the pain inflicted on someone by killing their loved ones. Just something to think about."

I nodded and returned with Das Ji, his words echoing in my head. Why did he tell me this? Amidst a string of thoughts playing in my head, it hit me. We had only pinned our suspicions on people who could've wanted to harm her, but not with who'd want to harm me.

Throughout the next week, I made a makeshift investigation board and posted pictures and details of people who would want to hurt me. I made several calls to Mr. Das for bits of information. I smoked and drank endlessly to ease the pain. When that didn't help, I screamed out loud amidst the four walls of my now empty house. Every cell in my body pushed me to keep going. Her fragrance haunted me. I even went to the café plaza near Neha's office where she spent time in the evening, just to feel the parts of her lingering in the corners of the world she had touched.

***

3 Days Later

I knocked on the door, and it opened immediately.

"Hey, hi!" She exclaimed, having been caught off guard.

"Hi Taaha," I grinned.

"What a pleasant surprise!"

"Am I going to be let in or are we exchanging pleasantries here itself?"

"I'm so sorry! Come in," she laughed, "What made you come here?"

"I was in the neighbourhood."

"I'll get some coffee for us." She went to the kitchen.

I snuck a glance in the living room and found a box in a corner.

"What are you doing?" She asked, coming in.

"Just looking around." I tried to sound nonchalant.

"Oh! Come, have a seat. I'll get something to eat." She handed me my coffee and went back.

"So Taaha, you never spoke about your family," I said casually, ending the call.

"You know I'm an orphan, right?" she said.

Just then, my phone rang. "Yes, Das Ji… Oh my god… I'm on my way… Thank you so much. What? How can it be? It's a woman?" I feigned astonishment. The clatter of utensils in the kitchen came to a halt. "I'll be right there."

I turned back to Taaha and resumed our conversation. "What about this?" I held up a photo which I had found in the corner. She appeared in the kitchen doorway. She was a small child in that photo, standing beside a man.

Her demeanour suddenly changed. Grabbing a knife, she came towards me, screaming, "He was my grandfather! You killed him. You killed him!" She attempted to stab me.

I held her arms down, took the knife from her, and sat her down. Just then, Das ji showed up with two female officers. "I was waiting for him the night of David's birthday party. He was walking from the railway station and you drove over him. Because of you, David is suffering. He told me everything. Grandpa was the only family I'd been left with. My parents died in a car accident. Grandpa was poor and couldn't provide for me, so he gave me to the orphanage when I was 9. I reached out when I was old enough and asked him to come and stay with me. He was overjoyed. But you killed him, all because of your drinking habits. I wanted to avenge his death, but I knew killing you would be futile. So, I chose her." She sneered at me through tears.

"I poisoned her, but that was too easy. I wasn't satisfied. So, I broke into your house and stabbed her incessantly. Mehta, the idiot, and I had an affair. I convinced him to kill her but he was too scared. He tried to stop me from breaking into your house, but he didn't know that she'd already been poisoned. I blackmailed him using our affair. That shut him up. But the next day, he said that he'd confess everything to the police. I had no other choice. He had to go. Luck favoured me when his wife and kids went out of town. He was drinking all day in his guest house. It made my job easy." There wasn't a single trace of remorse in her tone.

The two female officers cuffed her and dragged her out.

"Kabir?" She turned to me before being taken away. I turned to look at her.

"Rot in hell." With that, she was gone.

"How did you find out?" Das ji asked.

"Hari. After pondering about what he'd said, I began to look into people who'd want to hurt me. I went to the café where Neha used to go. The manager knew Neha well. He said that she was with a lady at around 7 p.m. the day she was murdered. I requested him to show the CCTV footage on that day, but conveniently enough, the CCTV wasn't working due to technical issues. By then, it was clear that the killer was a woman and must've poisoned Neha's drink. I grew more determined. None of the people I spoke to seemed to have a convincing motto. I gathered all the files about the accident case from you in which David and I were involved. I never forgot driving over that old man. Taaha had spoken only once about a grandfather, but I wanted to confirm.

"I went to her orphanage home and spoke with the head there. She confirmed that Taaha was given to them by a man. I showed her the old man's photo from the case files. 'Yes, that's him, but he was younger at that time,' she had said. I called you and shared my plan with you. Nair thought he'd seen Mehta speaking with Neha, but it had been Taaha." I finished.

"Great. The case is closed, then," he said.

"Not yet, Das Ji," I shook my head, "If Taaha is going to be penalized for killing two people, I'm equally guilty."

He remained silent for a few minutes. "As per the law, you're right. But David sacrificed his life for you years ago. His life's already been ruined. You've suffered enough, Kabir. Let the truth be untold." He patted my shoulder.

"Das Ji, it makes me no different than Taaha."

"It does, Kabir. She may be right to want to seek revenge, but her approach was wrong. You're going to suffer from loneliness anyway. I don't need to penalise you."

With that, Mr. Das left. Despite his assuring words, I knew that as long as I was alive, there would be no difference between my life and Taaha's. And with that realisation, I went home and looked forward to a life of loneliness.

13

WARD NO. 20

by Salbaz Sayyed

The semester was over, and we finally had a long vacation to look forward to. As my parents were out of town, my friends got busy making plans for the summer. That meant parties, crashing on the couch, late-night rides, and takeout food. That night, my friend Amit and I decided to go on a long ride at around 11:00 pm. We had some fun along the way, stopped by a few *dhabas*, and feasted on street-food. It was a specialty of Mumbai.

While riding, we saw a bike heading towards us, tires screeching against the asphalt. The headlights whooshed from one side to another, and we were almost blinded by the fast movement. Oh my god… Was he…? "Oh my god, Amit, he is drunk," I yelled, but it was too late. He rammed into our bike and I was thrown off by the collision. The last thing I remembered was the sound of an ambulance, some men, and then pitch darkness.

After a few hours, I awoke amidst four white walls, my vision blurry. It smelled like medicine everywhere. Hospital, I thought to myself. With a clouded vision, I could see a figure in white uniform walk up to my bedside and start bandaging my leg. Every bone in my body hurt. Turning my neck over to the side, I saw Amit sitting beside me. It took me a while to figure out his face with a hazy sight like that. Taking my hand and holding it tight, he said, "Never give up, okay? You'll be just fine." His words made me feel at ease. Just before I could utter a word or process what he'd said, I passed out again, seeing the nurse leave just a little hazily.

I don't remember how long I'd been asleep because I woke up with a throbbing headache and heavy eyes. I felt like I hadn't moved forever. Amit was still sitting beside me. He kept saying the same thing over and over again, "Don't give up, man. Hold on a little longer." The nurse entered again to check my pulse and skimmed through a few reports she was carrying. The doctor followed her in, his face impassive, giving nothing away. I couldn't read him at all. He stepped closer to the bed. "Sayed, I'm afraid we have some bad news for you," he said in a deep voice. Oh no. He continued, "We have contacted your parents already, but your friend… He died in the accident."

I felt my insides turn numb with shock. I turned over to my bedside where Amit had been sitting a few seconds ago. There was no one. "But Doctor, he was right here, talking to me. He was sitting here on this chair," I said pointing towards my bedside. "You can ask the nurse. She was here too. She must've heard him while she was bandaging my leg."

The nurse frowned at me, then at the doctor, puzzled. "No, Doctor, I was all alone," she said in a grim tone. I started panicking. I couldn't believe it. Had I been hallucinating? But how could it be? I could feel him holding my hand. My mind was reeling with having so much to process, and I could barely stay up. I drifted off to sleep again.

I woke up in a few hours, sweating. Tears pooled in my eyes. The more it hit me, the more I found it hard to believe. Amit was gone and it was entirely my fault. It felt like a part of me had just been ripped off. Just then, I heard voices in the hall. "Yes, he is here on this floor, ward no. 20." "Thank You." Maa and Papa. I could recognise their voices. Taking the wall's support, I stood up and walked towards the washroom. At that moment, I heard my ward door open and close. Assuming it was the nurse, I walked into the washroom without turning back.

When I came out, I stopped in my tracks. The nurse wasn't to be seen anywhere, but an old, shabby woman sat on the side of my bed. Wondering who she was, I managed to sputter out with the little bit of energy I had, "Hello, ma'am. I think you must have stepped in the wrong ward. This is my ward, number 20." She didn't respond. I tiptoed closer to her. She looked pretty depressed. Her hospital clothes were dirty and had almost worn off. She kept staring at the floor with her shabby hair running down to her waist. She must've been traumatized, staying here for a long time. Poor woman.

"Hello, ma'am," I said, louder this time, hoping for a reaction. She finally looked up at me. There were big, dark circles under her eyes, and her lips were all cracked. Her skin was dry. "Here, let me pour you a glass of water," I smiled sympathetically. I turned towards the little side table, and picking up the jar, began to pour water. Just then, I heard a weird sound behind me. I ignored it and kept pouring, assuming it was from the other ward. Hospitals were weird.

Just as I was about to turn, I heard the noise again, only louder this time. I glanced at my bed. The woman wasn't there anymore. That's when I heard a strange growl. I was beginning to get a little scared. My eyes darted around frantically in search of the old lady. My hands trembled and I began to perspire. Looking around, I couldn't see her anywhere. She must've gone back, I thought, turning back to the table. And there she was, standing right in front of me, her bloodshot eyes blazing with rage.

It seemed like her jaw had dropped sideways. I stood there, petrified. I couldn't move an inch from where I stood. She came closer, and a stench filled the room. It was of dead, decaying, rotten meat. She suddenly began to yell, "Why didn't you save me? Why did you leave me alone?" Her sharp shrill pierced my ears, startling me. It was like I couldn't look away, even if I wanted to. She pounced on me, and we landed on the chair, her nails digging into my skin. She grabbed my collar and went on saying the same thing repeatedly. I tried to scream and yell, but to no avail. My voice was stuck in my throat. I looked into her eyes one last time before losing consciousness.

The next morning, when I opened my eyes, I felt more relieved than ever. What a nightmare, I thought to myself. I looked sideways to find my parents with their eyes fixated on me. It seemed like they had been waiting for me to wake up for a long time. I told them about my dream, and asked about Amit, hoping he had survived too. They didn't respond, but instead, tore away their gaze.

Just then, the nurse walked in. "You don't have to worry now. You're safe. We will be shifting you to the other ward soon." I looked at her, puzzled. I was completely lost in terms of what she was referring to. "Maa, what happened?" I asked, turning towards my mother, who was blankly looking into my eyes. Then, she said, in a rather low voice, "Papa and the nurse saved you, beta." She continued, her voice quivering, "You ran upstairs, hovering over the edge of the roof, about to end your life."

My eyes widened. I didn't remember any of it. I looked at the nurse, who told me, "There were always rumours about a lady who died here about a year ago. She was a psychopath and a cold-blooded killer who was admitted here before she breathed her last. She had seven sons and not one came to see her when she was ill. We have reason to believe that she targeted the lives of seven youngsters who reminded her of her children. Within the last year, five young boys, sometimes men, who had been here, had suddenly committed suicides. Your friend, Amit, was driven to suicide as well. You were supposed to be the seventh." It took me a while to process what she was saying. With every word she spoke, my eyes widened in horror.

"We will seal this room. You'll be safe now," she said, wheeling in a wheelchair and helping me over it. I got myself seated.

"Are you sure?" I asked in a nervous tone.

"Yes. Now, you need to focus on getting better."

She escorted my parents out to the waiting area in the lobby and shifted me to the next ward. As she wheeled me in and placed me in the new bed, I requested her to bring me a glass of water. She went to the bedside table and poured a glass. I couldn't figure out if it was my imagination or not, but I began to hear weird sounds once again. I shrugged it off as an effect of last night's trauma, but when the nurse turned towards me, I realized I was looking into a familiar pair of blood-shot eyes. No. As she slowly closed in on me, the same air filled the room once again, and the familiar stench of rotten meat surrounded me before I passed out one last time, this time into a never-ending sleep.

14

THE HIDDEN PREDATOR

by Darshini Parthiban

It was a Friday afternoon and a slow day at the station. With no new cases, Maya D'Souza was seated on her desk and scrolling through her news app. It was filled with outrage over the Hathras gang-rape case. Another day, another victim of the chauvinistic patriarchal society. She shook her head in dismay. As she was mulling over the news, Inspector Vikram called her over.

"Detective D'Souza, we have a new one. A famous professor at IISC, Bangalore, was found dead in his house in Koramangla yesterday. It appears to be suicide, but apparently, the professor had a conflict with his colleague in the afternoon on the same day. There's an ongoing debate among the students suspecting foul play. The case has been handed over to the CB-CID, the details of which have been mailed to you. Get ready, we're leaving," he said.

Leaving his cabin, Maya checked her mail. The victim was her father's neighbour, Professor Vincent Paul. He had been found dead in his bathroom, bleeding from the cut on his wrists. She checked the pictures from the forensics. His body lay in the bathtub. There were two deep slits on each of his wrists. The blade was lying on the floor near the tub. There had been no signs of forced entry into the apartment. He had been alone at the time of his death.

Three people were listed a prime suspects. When she reviewed the list, she was horrified. One was his wife Leela, his colleague with whom he was not on good terms, Aadhi, and finally, Maya's own brother, Rohan.

She couldn't picture her 15-year-old introverted brother as a suspect in a murder case. They weren't that close. They used to be, but when she was fifteen, their mother had died in an accident. After her death, their family had slowly drifted apart. Their father, a successful entrepreneur, immersed himself in work. Rohan was too young then. Not being able to look after them both, Maya was sent to boarding school. She used study as distraction. After training in Krav-Maga, she joined the CB-CID after finishing college and moved into an apartment closer to the station.

Vincent had moved into the apartment next door with his wife soon after their mother's death.

Pondering over the interesting turn of events, Maya reviewed the details. All three suspects were the only ones who had visited the apartment the previous evening. Rohan had visited and left at around 5 p.m. when the professor was alone, but Rohan was just next door the whole time. Leela, who had been out when Rohan had visited, returned home at 6 p.m. Aadhi had come at around 7 p.m. The wife and the friend had left the apartment around 8.30 p.m.

Interestingly, they both had left together. The death was reported at 10:34 p.m. The CCTV in the building hadn't been working for over a week. Someone had leaked the news about the professor's death, which had spread like wildfire. Students demanded justice for their beloved professor.

Reaching the crime scene, Maya looked around the apartment. The forensics had done a good job and had documented everything. There was nothing new. They were discussing the next procedure outside the apartment when Rohan came out from his.

"Didi, what are you doing here?" he asked, rather taken aback.

"The better question is, what were you doing in Vincent's apartment yesterday? I thought you were supposed to be on your school trip!" Maya said sternly.

"The trip ended early, so I came back yesterday in the afternoon."

Not wanting to probe him in front of Vikram, Maya bid him goodbye and left.

Back at the station, Maya and Vikram did a background check on Vincent. A promising student from a young age, he had topped both JEE and KVPY exams and joined IISC, Bangalore. Passing out as a gold medallist, he went on to complete his Ph.D. Finally, four years ago, he became a professor at his alma mater. Adored by his students and colleagues, and with remarkable academic achievements, he had been quite successful professionally. Gone too soon at 37!

Maya and Vikram went over to review the statements collected by the police the previous day. Rohan hadn't given a statement as their father had been away on a business trip.

In Leela's statement, Vincent had been more antsy than usual that evening. He was an alcoholic and was prone to outbursts. She became scared. Then Aadhi had come for their weekly dinner, during which, Vincent had been agitated and had picked a verbal spat with Aadhi, after which Aadhi had left. Leela had gone out to send him off. She had then wandered around the neighbourhood for an hour or so before she returned home to find Vincent dead in a pool of his own blood in the bathroom.

In Aadhi's statement, he had arrived home after dinner, only to receive a call about Vincent's death an hour later. The rest of his statement matched Leela's.

The autopsy report arrived. The time of death was around 10 to 11 p.m. It said that Vincent had died of profuse blood loss from his cuts. The blade had only Vincent's prints on it. Having no new developments in the case, they decided to call it a night.

Maya went and confronted her brother. "I know you're innocent, but there might be evidence against you. I know you might feel that there are things that you cannot share. But I won't judge you. Tell me the truth so I can help you."

Rohan broke down and opened up. Three years ago, at the cusp of adolescence, he'd felt very lonely and their father had been busy with work. That was when Vincent started paying attention to him. He was so nice. He called Rohan over whenever they were alone. Slowly, he changed. He started offering Rohan cocaine. Not wanting to offend him, Rohan accepted it and soon got addicted. Vincent then started asking him unusual favours in return, which soon turned sexual. Fed up, Rohan stopped asking him for cocaine 8 months ago. Vincent was furious. A few months ago, he started blackmailing Rohan, threatening to expose his addiction. On the night of his death, he had invited Rohan over to blackmail him.

"I was done. I told him to go ahead because I had stopped caring. I just wanted to escape from him. I could never kill him," said Rohan, his vulnerability on the brim. He looked positively scared. Maya listened in shell-shocked in silence with tears in her eyes. She felt ashamed of herself for abandoning her brother. Not anymore. She consoled him saying, "It's alright. We'll overcome this."

Just then, a voice cried out, "Oh, my god! What have I done?"

They turned to see their father standing there, looking shocked and remorseful. He had arrived home from his trip, after missing yet another important happening of their lives.

"After your mother's death, I didn't know how to look after you. Your mother was brilliant at that. I thought the only way around was to focus on my job and make sure you were well provided for. I was wrong. I should've paid more attention to both of you. I should have been a better father. As for Vincent, it's a good thing he's dead or I would've killed him myself! I know it's too little, too late, but I hope you'll forgive me," he said regretfully.

"It is too late," Maya said flatly, "I hope at least now you'll pay more attention to what goes on in your own house than the stock market."

Her father apologised profusely. He had abandoned them when they needed him the most, but he was trying to make amends. She accepted his apology. After all, they had to start somewhere. She turned to Rohan.

"Do you have any evidence of his blackmail with you?"

"No, it's there on his laptop. He never sent me any text or letter about it."

"At the interview, say exactly as I tell you." Maya told him the details and left.

The next morning, forensics sent over Vincent's laptop after hacking it. Maya and Vikram opened it to find the screensaver of Joker with the quote, *"Some men just want to watch the world burn."* Indeed. On searching his mail, they found nothing incriminating. No evidence of Rohan's addiction or his feud with Aadhi.

There were a few journal entries. In his recent ones, he had written about his alcohol addiction and how it made him act out. He had written how his wife didn't understand him and felt distant. His best friend was jealous of him. There were days where he had almost ended it in a moment's decision.

Reading the entries, Vikram said, "If this isn't suicide, it could be that Leela and Aadhi paired up and killed him. Let's think about it over the weekend. On Monday, we'll interview all the suspects."

Everything was coming together. Maya sincerely hoped that the case would soon close. Monday morning arrived. Maya's father accompanied Rohan to the police station. Six hours later, all the suspects were gathered in the investigation room. Rohan, on her request, had told nothing of his addiction and abuse. He had only told that he frequented Vincent's house for clarifying doubts. That day was just another day and nothing special had happened.

Leela talked about their relationship. He had been a perfect gentleman when they had met but had changed after their marriage. He turned controlling and aggressive, often had bouts of depression, and soon became an alcoholic. The past few months, his behaviour had become more erratic. There was despair in her tone over his loss. Vikram asked her whether Vincent had ever physically abused her. Although Leela said no, her eyes said otherwise.

Aadhi said that he'd been Vincent's friend since college. He had noticed his psychotic behaviour at times, with its manic and depressive phases. He never got treated for it, being too proud for his own good. He had been there when Leela had met Vincent. After their marriage, he noticed his controlling attitude towards Leela and often enquired after her. After he'd joined the IISC as his colleague four years ago, there were weekly dinners at his house every Thursday. They usually didn't cancel it except for an emergency. That night, he'd been quite agitated during the dinner, but nothing else happened.

When Vikram asked him about their feud, he said it was nothing but a difference of opinion over one of their research papers. It was over nothing, and it hadn't created a rift between them. But it was in public, so many people had noticed it.

After the interrogation, they seemed to have hit a dead-end. With increasing proof that Vincent was indeed psychotic and depressed, it was becoming clear that he had indeed killed himself, giving in to one of his suicidal impulses. The case was investigated for two more weeks before it was finally closed off as suicide.

A month later, Maya was sitting at her desk. Her phone pinged. It was a message from her father. She smiled. He had been trying hard the past few weeks, trying to make amends.

She thought back to the day six months ago, where it all had begun. It was during one of her rare visits home. She hated being there after what had happened so far. She had dinner with her family and had left, only to return to get her forgotten keys from the apartment. That was when she heard that monster blackmailing her brother.

She realized with horror what had happened. Having been a victim of Vincent herself, she felt sick that she hadn't seen the signs in Rohan. After being sent away following her mother's death, she had felt lonely. During her visits home, Vincent had sniffed the loneliness like a predator sensing its prey. He'd lured her in the same way he had Rohan. He had violated her body. She had known it was wrong, but she felt too ashamed to speak out. She kept mum and steered clear of him during her visits home. Going back there always brought back the memories. So, she avoided it altogether, going only a handful of times over the years, immersing herself in studies.

She had never imagined Rohan would fall prey to him. Vincent didn't care about the gender of his victims. He was a pedophile. A pervert. A pathetic human being.

So, Maya decided to rid the earth of Vincent. She started following every move of his over the next few months. She saw how he was preying on her innocent brother. She wanted to kill him there and then, but she bided her time. She saw the fight between him and Aadhi, realizing she could use it to her advantage. So she had chosen the weekly dinner for the day of the murder. Her brother and father were supposed to be out of town on that day.

She knew Leela liked to walk around the neighbourhood when Vincent was in one of his moods. To make sure Vincent was agitated that evening, she had sent him an anonymous letter stating she had evidence about his abusive behaviour and that she was going to release it soon. It had worked.

After Aadhi and Leela left, she went to the apartment. Seeing her, he smiled condescendingly, asking if she was thirsty for another round of what he had done to her. Her sixteen-year-old self would have been scared, but not anymore. She had smiled like a predator at its prey. She lured him into the bathroom and subdued him with a strike to his neck, careful not to leave any signs or marks which would indicate that he had been struck. She put him in his bathtub, slit his wrists, and waited. By the time he gained consciousness, it was too late. He had lost too much blood and had become weak. As he looked at her with frightened eyes, she stood there, watching him as light went out of his eyes. She also erased all the evidence of Rohan's addiction from his laptop and planted some suicidal entries in his journal.

She had also spread the news of his death around the college campus, planting the idea that Aadhi might be a suspect, creating an uproar among the students. As expected, the case was handed over to the CB-CID from the police. Having been a workaholic all those years had paid off, and as she had predicted, she was given the case. She had also wanted to make sure Leela was not suspected. She was as much a victim of Vincent as Maya and Rohan. The only thing that went awry in her plan was

Rohan's early return. Fortunately, she was able to manipulate and close the case.

Coming back to the present, she messaged her dad asking about Rohan's rehabilitation. He had been doing well. So had Leela, although she did mourn her abusive husband now and then. They had been happy since that leech had been out of their lives.

Maya looked at the stack of cases waiting for her. She prepared for her next case, ready to serve justice.

15

ROBINSON MURDER

by Himanshu Sukhala

J oseph Robinson died on 20th June and was buried at the Robinson family grave alongside his long-departed mother. The sad affair was attended by family and select close friends. The noteworthy attendees were: Gibralt Robinson, the father of the deceased, Cecilia Robinson, the wife in black silk attire, Gregor and John Robinson, the older and younger brothers respectively, and the 22-year-old son of the deceased, Joseph Jr. The incident would have been just that, had not John Robinson been found dead with a bullet through his neck to prove it on the eve of his brother's funeral, in front of the Town Hall's staircase where several by-standers had heard him shouting, "The bastard did it... Damn it!"

Detective Connor sat at his desk, scratching his curled up overgrown beard with his pen, looking at the picture of the body of John Robinson with a bullet through his neck. He wanted to crack and finish it up as quickly as possible so that he could go for on the vacation he had put his leave application for at the captain's desk.

The whole city knew that the Robinson family's wealth came from its connection with the mafia, but no one had ever been able to put the puzzle into place for them to serve time. So the sudden news of the deaths of two of the members from the mafia was pretty big for the police department, but the last words of the youngest brother had aroused suspicions about the death of Joseph Robinson, too. Connor had written down the list of possible suspects on the notepad in front of him based on motive.

The first one was the widow, Cecilia, who, as rumours would have it, was known to be nosy in the mafia business. But if John's last words were to be believed, the perpetrator was male, so that put a wrench in the gears on this line of suspicion. Second on the list was the only brother left, suspected of wanting to get all of the money, and the third one was Gagaron Somwell, the only man to rival the Robinson family's power in the underworld.

"So did you get any headway on the Robinson case?"

Connor looked up to find his fellow detective, Leslie Donwood, standing over his head. He had a short burly beard and, as usual, reeked of cigarettes.

"Nah, but I have some suspects here. My gut says it was a mob hit, probably by Somwell's crew."

"Now, now, you better have some proof before you start making allegations openly, or are you so naïve to think he won't have ears in the police department? If you go on like this, your gut won't be able to say much with a knife stuck in it."

"Yeah, I hear you. Are you going home or you going to help?"

"Well, the missus is on periods so there ain't much to do at home."

"Then get your ass down and help me go through these autopsy files. Here, you take Joseph's, while I go get the ballistics report on the bullet which did in the younger brother."

Connor knew the autopsy reports were straight and concise. Joseph died from an anaphylactic shock which was triggered by some sort of allergen, but it may as well have been an accident, as he did have a history of allergies, and it was pollen season this time of year. The younger brother's was even more simplistic, a bullet through the neck usually does the trick for most humans.

"Detective Connor, there you are, here for the bullet that did John Robinson in?"

"Yes Gerald, good evening, anything noteworthy in this?"

"Standard issue .22 calibre. So much of it out there that it's practically impossible to trace."

Connor groaned and nodded to the man behind the fence before heading back to his desk to find Leslie grinning from side to side and waving a file at him.

"Did you know Joseph Jr. is not a legitimate child?"

"Yes, they adopted him into the family, Mrs. Robinson was pregnant when she married, right?"

"And 'the bastard did it' doesn't ring any bells?"

"I checked into him, he was with the old man when the shooting took place, and I really don't think he would have the guts to kill his own father. Plus, he was already on the will so he had no motive, too."

"Still, you can never know what these scums are thinking in their minds. Anything in the ballistics?"

"Absolute nada."

"Well, it's 3 o'clock in the morning. I say we take a nap and then start with the alibis at dawn."

"Nothing to do till morning, anyway."

Connor woke up and had a cold shower before putting on the same clothes he wore yesterday. He started walking towards the police station, thinking how to close the file before the day's end so that he could catch his vacation flight when he bumped into Leslie coming from the station's direction in a hurry.

"Why the rush, Leslie?"

"You didn't hear? The older Robinson brother got into a collision early in the morning and got away with just a warning from The Reaper."

Leslie stopped and tried to gather his breathing while Connor hailed a cab and gave the driver the directions. The Robinson Manor was huge, and by huge, it meant a three-storeyed Vatican style mansion on 18 acres of land. Connor rang up the front gate at the manor, and after announcing himself to the guard, made his way to the front door followed by Leslie trailing behind. Junior was at the door waiting for them, and after an exchange of pleasantries, they made their way to the drawing room on the left end of the hall. Gibralt Robinson was already there sitting at the head of the oval table and motioned them to sit on the couch.

He looked like a sage from old fairy tales - heavily wrinkled face, thinning grey hairline, and deep eyes filled with time itself. Losing two sons in such a short time can do that to a person I guess, thought Connor.

"I wouldn't take much of your time, Mr. Robinson, sir. I'd like to ask for the whereabouts of you and your family yesterday."

"You think we did this to our own family?" interrupted Junior.

"Calm down, Junior. They're just doing their job."

Connor hadn't even noticed Junior in the room. He glanced towards Leslie and gestured to him to take his hand off his weapon. Junior had alarmed him with his outburst. Although Connor sympathized with the reaction, something nudged his mind at that moment, which he couldn't place a finger on.

"So, sir, where were you after the funeral yesterday?"

"We all came back to the house and some friends and acquaintances were here to give their condolences. After that, I was with John in my study room till about 4 in the evening, and then took a stroll around the house till the news came in."

"Were you alone while you took a walk?"

"No, he wasn't. I was with him the whole time. I thought the last interrogation would stay in your mind at least for a couple of days," growled Junior.

Connor peeked over his shoulder at Junior still standing at the front of the entrance, angry. Leslie asked Mr. Robinson if he had any suspicions on someone or something unusual he had noticed with John that day, only to get answered in the negative.

"Well, we would like to meet Mrs. Robinson, too, so if you could ask her to come here?"

"Junior, go bring your mother," ordered Gibralt.

Junior looked at the detectives and left the room. The drawing room was large, with two sets of couches around the oval table, and the leather armchair on which Mr. Robinson was sitting.

"I am sorry sir, but you know we have to check and recheck everything."

"Don't pay heed to his words. He is a young one; once this is well behind him, I am going to put that fool into Cambridge and away from this town."

"Sir if you have anything that might hel-"

Leslie was interrupted by the sound of Mrs. Robinson's footsteps, who was still in her mourning dress. An elegant woman, she was aware of the impact of her presence in a room. Connor had experienced such types and knew how dangerous they could be. Leslie would've seconded it too. She walked up to the head of the family and stood on the side of the armchair while Junior resumed his position at the entrance.

"I am sorry for your loss, Mrs. Ro-"

"I was with my aunt and sister after the funeral. You can talk to them if you want. They are in the guest room upstairs. If that's all, I will excuse myself, Detective."

Damn it, woman! At least let a man finish his sentence, thought Leslie, before jotting down the information in his pad. He glanced at his partner meekly. He knew that their alibis had been checked before and the expressions on Connor told the same story – they were headed nowhere.

"Would you gentlemen like some tea? I am sorry, I forgot my manners. We have sweetened peaches too, I grew them all my own."

"Thank you very much, Mr. Robinson, sir, but we have someplace to be. We'll take our leave now. Sorry for your loss. Ma'am, Junior." The detectives tipped their hats to the lady of the house and went towards the front door, accompanied by Junior who was still scowling till they left the porch of the house.

"So where do we start now?"

"How's Gregor doing?"

"ICU. His right arm had to be amputated, crushed under the wreck. He is out of the mafia business, that's for sure. Doctors are saying he hit his head hard too."

"Not much for us, then, is it? But something's been troubling me ever since we found John down at the Town Hall. What was he doing up there?"

"Apparently, he had some property records that he had filed for at the hall. I reckon they are still there."

"Let's find out if they were worth a bullet in the neck."

A blonde receptionist was sitting at the front desk of Town Hall when the detectives reached there.

"You're pretty early here, Susan. Keeping the boss-man happy?" Leslie smirked.

"Same goes for you, Leslie, but one of us had a bath before heading out."

"Now, Mrs. Donwood, I agree with you on the latter," piped in Connor, "But we're here on official business. Could you retrieve the property records that John Robinson filed for and bring them to us?"

"Alright. You two wait here. I'll be back in a moment."

While Mrs. Donwood was gone to get the records, Leslie looked at Connor like a child who has just been betrayed by his brother.

"Here you go, Connor. Keep his paws off them. Don't want to stink up the whole file cabinet, do we?" teased Susan.

"Yes, ma'am."

Back at the police department, Connor shuffled through them while Leslie went on to get some much-needed bad coffee. Over a dozen of the property records were pretty new, so Connor separated them into two piles, leaving the old ones for Leslie to dig into, while he checked the latest records. Connor opened the first file, read through the title, the name of the corresponding property, the individuals involved, and shut it. He hurriedly opened the next, then the next, and didn't stop till he had picked, opened, and thrown them all on his desk. He quickly opened his file drawer, pulled out the autopsy reports, and checked the cause of death for Joseph Robinson. Anaphylactic shock. He then pulled the medical history of the man and glanced through the known allergens. Leslie came back with two cups of coffee and placed them on the desk while he grabbed his chair to sit and dig through his own pile.

"Well you know, Connor, I think that these Robinsons are better dead. The old man had worked hard to establish the factory in town while his sons played gangsters. Junior will finally get out of the crooked life. Hey, you listening to me?"

Leslie looked up from the file to find a flabbergasted Connor.

"Hey, you alright?" Leslie asked while an officer in uniform came up to the desk and informed them that Gibralt Robinson had suffered a heart attack due to old age and passed on while being rushed to the hospital.

"Damn shame. The man worked hard and suffered too. Right, Connor?"

Connor looked at Leslie with a smile on his face which was part sarcastic and part pitiful and passed on the marked files towards Leslie. He picked up the files and read them. When he was done, he looked up to find Connor sighing and packing his belongings to get to his much-needed vacation.

The property records showed that old man Robinson had transferred all the mafia dealings to a Mr. Somwell in exchange for a college trust and an "out-of-court agreement". Joseph Robinson's medical history listed peaches as a potential high-risk allergen.

16

MURDER AT HAPPYVILLE

by Anamika Kundu

The morning papers reported it in small print somewhere between a lost horse and a stolen car on page 13, or was it page 14? The dead body of Mr. So-and-so was found in the parking lot outside a huge, popular departmental store.

Only a few people bothered to read it. Then there was another body in another parking lot. Apparently, during peak hours, a man was shot dead in the busy parking area of a prominent grocery store.

This report grabbed eyes. The residents of Happyville sat up and took note, the reporter was happy, and the TV reporters sniffed it out. Seemed like it was just the thing. After all, life in mundane homes had been missing a bit of drama.

The next day, the front pages were rife with another murder - same modus operandi. The police were interviewed; the reporters turned detective – a la Sherlock Holmes! Sniffing and digging, they concluded the suspect was a pretty tall Caucasian.

"Wait!" said the TV news, "It is a short and coloured man!" On the other hand, the police said, "Please, let us do our jobs. We cannot say anything yet!"

The town was abuzz and the sheriff was on one channel after the other, trying to calm down people and warning the perpetrator that his identity was quite clear and he would soon be hunted down.

Now, the people were completely shaken up. He seemed like a ghost, a person who came from nowhere, killed his unsuspecting victims, and disappeared only he knew where. Responsible parents would not leave their children and venture out, and responsible adults wouldn't dare to leave their senile parents by themselves.

The only car in a 500-car parking lot drew the attention of a TV reporter. "Sir, when no one dares to venture out, how come you have come here? What is your reason to be so brave?"

"Oh! You see if I have to die, I will die! We are born with a pre-determined number of breaths after all. Haven't you heard of the Karma theory?"

Now, the criminal thought of taking the drama up a notch. This time, his choice of victim was a female of ethnic origin. After the deed, he placed a tarot card neatly near the body. He tossed a coin between 10 of Swords and 5 of Pentacles. It was to be 5 of Pentacles. All hell broke loose.

The police claimed their investigations were back to square one. The sheriff said he had no clue who could have committed such a heinous series of crimes. The reward for any information regarding the perpetrator was straight away increased ten-fold.

Oh, the dark depths of the human mind! The panellists on TV shows discussed, questioned, and pounced on each other. A few homies turned up at the police station, describing a stranger at the last crime scene. What made matters worse was that the sketch the artist drew showed a different man every time. So much for placing a reward on the criminal's head!

The newspapers were soon joined by weekly magazines. Everyone wanted to make a quick buck from 'The Flavour of the Season'. Attendance dipped in schools, colleges, and offices. The usual chatter of Happyville had turned down to hush-hush between children and adults.

The unknown stranger was once again being built up, and a bit of shape, motive, and background was added to conjure up an identity. He, too, seemed to play along, dropping interesting tarot cards next to his victims. As time passed by, he seemed to grow bolder. He wilfully played along with every speculation. One could picture him laughing gleefully. Or could the suspect be she?

As the number of victims kept increasing, it became evident that he or she was a well-trained sharpshooter. The bullets indicated it was a sniper. So finally, 'The Sniper' had an identity.

Fear loomed large. People looked at their neighbours and wondered 'Is he The Sniper?' 'Is the lady with the warm smile The Sniper?' 'Could my neighbour be The Sniper?' Meanwhile, officers Thomas and Roy searched for evidence. They traced the tarot cards to a manufacturer from New York. Finally, a lead. Thomas went up to New York, and on questioning, gathered that someone from Happyville named John Preacher had bought a pack online.

The following day, Roy and Thomas looked up the address of Preacher. There were six individuals with that name. They made a list of all the addresses. It was going to be a long day so they split up and went to investigate.

One lived in a cubbyhole and could barely move from his couch to the door. The second one was a respectable Math teacher in a secondary school. The third had moved out of town. The fourth was a young man who had moved to Chicago to pursue higher studies and had not been in town for more than 2 months. The fifth was a respected veteran, who had lost his child and spouse. The sixth one had passed away just a month ago.

So now, they narrowed down their list of suspects to the Math teacher, the young man in university at Chicago, and the respected veteran.

The police department wondered how many people were part of this expert shooting team. They tried to calculate how the shooters must have moved from one location to another without being detected, and how they remained untraceable. The sheriff was having sleepless nights and ensured everyone else did too. They were overworked and severely understaffed.

It had been a hard day, and they had hardly made any headway in 'The Sniper Case'. Officer Thomas was passing by on a lonely stretch of road when his senses started tingling. With many speculations, the newspaper reporters hounding them, and tempers soaring, everyone was exasperated. But what were his senses telling him? There was nothing in front of him or behind. He stopped his car and looked around. Inhaling deeply, he stepped out, senses all alert, radio on the ready for a quick call if required. That's when he saw it. A partially hidden blue sedan, with its boot visible. "This is the police! Is anyone there? Can I help you?" Silence. He switched on the powerful searchlight and radioed for help. There was something very much out of place here.

Officer Roy reached the spot in just a few minutes. Together, they checked the car. No papers, documents – nothing. As they turned, they could see the parking lot of a huge hardware store some 600-700 metres away on the other side of the road. The place of the last murder. "That's it," said Roy, excited. They took the car down to the police station. When they opened the boot, they shared a look mixed with shock and victory. Some space had been created, along with a blanket and a cushion, for someone to lie there comfortably.

The horizon was turning a light pink as the dawn of a new day hovered to take over. Chief Charlie was peering at them through his glasses. He did not seem happy. As Thomas briefed him, Roy noticed a small hole which seemed to have been recently carved into the metal of the boot, like a peephole. They looked at the blanket and cushion again. Yes, someone had lain there all right. There was an impression of a long object being placed on it, too. As they searched every inch of the car, they found a folded scrap of paper. It was a bill in the name of Daniel Preacher from Boulevard, Happyville.

The name sounded familiar, thought Thomas. Wracking his brain, he couldn't understand where he had read it. Then, it suddenly struck him. He and Roy checked out the obituaries of the last three months, and there it was. Daniel Preacher had died in an accident with his mother three months ago. That was why the sedan was untraceable. The killer had been driving a dead boy's car.

Roy and Thomas informed Chief Charlie that they knew who it was. There was evidence of two people being in the car. The cushion was used to support a long-barrelled gun – a sniper. They put the address under surveillance. The phone on his desk rang, "Chief Charlie," he said and his expression visibly changed. Barely being able to keep the phone properly back, he yelled, "Let's go boys, we've got him!" They drove like hell, with no sirens. On arrival, the chief gave the signal and the SWAT teams burst in.

On searching the house, they found the rooms empty, barring the kitchen and two bedrooms. The backyard, though, was another story. A firing range had been created and regular shooting practice seemed to be carried out there. An obstacle course, too, had been created, fit to train marines. Roy and

Thomas looked at each other and couldn't resist giving each other fist bumps.

Thomas got copies of John Preacher's driving licence from the house and the photograph was soon shared. Meanwhile, Roy had done a complete background check and come up with the fact that Preacher was a veteran, and highly respected for his sharp-shooting and gentle behaviour. They soon tracked Preacher and his accomplice to a seedy bar. As the SWAT team charged in, they were baffled.

Preacher, a middle-aged veteran, tall, muscled, and calm whereas his accomplice, Jeff, a younger, twenty-something, seemed shocked at the intrusion. Preacher quickly regained composure, but the shouts and screams of the younger man were a great testimony.

Handcuffed and taken to the police station, they admitted they were 'The Snipers' and had committed all the murders.

The reporters had a field day at the press release.

It was in the special edition of the newspapers the next day. 'The Sniper' was caught at last. Glorious tributes were paid to the Police department, Thomas, and Roy in particular.

The investigations revealed Preacher was a shooting expert and held in high esteem in the Army and among his colleagues. After losing his wife and son, his only family, he had become rather withdrawn. In a fit of anger, he wanted to hurt people, especially those he thought were happy.

The peaceful, tree-lined neighbourhood could not believe it. They'd had a cold-blooded murderer amidst them, yet they never had an inkling. In fact, he happened to be one of the most respected people as he never hurt anyone, neither did he raise his voice. Well, such is the human mind – an enigma!

17

A TRYSTED CRIME

by Kristin Carmen

It wasn't long after the class reunion that Amena received the call. It was her husband, Varum. He had to leave the reunion early for work at the hospital. It wasn't like him to call from work, and he sounded upset.

"Amena, I'm afraid I have some bad news for you," he said painstakingly. "It's about your friend Aasha whom we saw earlier at the reunion." Amena could hear him struggling to choose the right words.

"What is it?" she asked, getting worried.

"She was murdered."

Amena went blank. Every sound around her muffled down. "Wait, what do you mean, she was murdered? We – I just saw her."

She couldn't wrap her head around the fact that her old best friend was dead, let alone murdered. "Amena, she's gone. I'm sorry. All I know is that she was bruised badly and died from knife wounds."

· Just then, Amena could hear her husband being paged over the hospital intercom to arrive at the Intensive Care Unit. Stat. She knew that seconds could mark the line of difference between life and death for patients in their care. She thanked and rushed Varum off the phone, then took the seat next to her in a daze. She couldn't believe that her best friend from high school had just been killed. Amena had only left Aasha's side a couple of hours ago.

That night they'd had an amazing time. Going down memory lane with her old friends had been heart-warming, and it felt like she was back in school again, regardless of how much their lives had changed. It reminded her how fortunate she was to have known so many wonderful people, and how important it was not to lose touch with those she had been close to in the past. She and Aasha had made it a point earlier that night to catch up later during the week and make it a regular habit to meet up. Now, she would never have a chance to reconnect with Aasha.

Amena couldn't imagine why anyone would want to harm Aasha, let alone kill her. It was beyond her comprehension. Aasha was one of those people whom everyone adored. Always kind and friendly, Aasha lit up the room wherever she went.

Amena needed to know more about what had happened. She decided that she would visit law enforcement in the morning to get more details. She had just been about to climb into bed when her husband had called to tell her the news.

Amena lay down but couldn't get it out of her head. If only she hadn't lost contact with Aasha, she would have known more about her life and those she associated with regularly, she thought woefully.

The next morning, Amena woke up and got ready to go out early. Varum still wasn't home from the night shift at the hospital, so she left him a note, explaining that she was going into the city for a while and would be back later.

She headed out the door, but the moment she got into her car, everything seemed to hit her all at once. She started to cry for her old friend. Everything seemed like a nightmare. A memorable evening followed by a horrible dream. Yet, Amena knew this wasn't a dream. It was a sad reality.

She parked a block from the police station and grabbed a quick kathi-roll from a street vendor along the way. Once in the police station, she found someone who could answer her questions. She had to bribe him into getting the information but succeeded in the end. They had a few leads to go by, but one, in particular, stood out.

Amena recalled that Aasha had received a phone call during the reunion that had seemed to startle her. Aasha wasn't exactly the type of person that became nervous easily, but the call had seemed to rattle her up. In a timorous voice, Aasha had explained, "That was my ex-boyfriend. He is always making odd requests when I am at functions." Then, she had just shaken her head as if to shake off what had happened. Then it was as if a light switch turned back on and she was all smiles again.

It had left Amena a little uneasy, but then again, it didn't seem like much at the time. According to the police, he had a key to her house, and suspiciously enough, a flimsy alibi. He was supposedly at a bar that evening and went straight home, but that particular bar closed at 2 a.m. It was at about the same time Amena said goodbye to Aasha and went home.

Amena asked to see the statement he made. With some bribery and with the help of a friend, they obliged. She read over the details of the case and all statements. Everyone but the ex-boyfriend had solid evidence of their whereabouts the previous evening.

According to the reports, Aasha sustained multiple bruises and several fatal stab wounds throughout her body. She was stabbed by a knife that was from her own kitchen. The police believed that she must have known the attacker because there were no signs of a break-in, nothing was stolen, and she had not been raped.

The report also stated that the neighbours heard screams from that direction and called the police. However, by the time the police and medics arrived, Aasha had bled too much from her injuries. At least Amena now had something to go by and memorized the name and address of the ex-boyfriend.

Amena thanked the police and quickly left the building to write down the name, address, and information so she wouldn't forget. She figured that she would do a little detective work on her own since she knew that law enforcement did not take the time to follow up with these matters.

Amena decided that she would check out Aasha's ex-boyfriend's house, hoping she could catch a glimpse of him. Luckily, that actually did happen. As she approached the house, he was getting out of his car. He was a large man but otherwise didn't look all that threatening. He smiled and waved at the little boy who lived next door, who waved back.

She gathered that the man had just come back to the house temporarily to get something before heading back to work, so she decided to park the car several streets away and come up with a plan. Maybe if she talked to some of the ladies in his neighbourhood, someone may give her a clue or two. After all, they would probably think that she worked for the police department undercover and not question her.

Half-an-hour later, Amena decided to try her luck. She drove by his house and was relieved to see that his car was gone. Perfect timing, she thought and smiled. She saw a lady about her age tending to a young child. Amena decided that would be a good opportunity to ask questions. She parked the car and headed towards the lady.

The lady was very friendly and greeted her with a smile. "Hello, are you lost? Can I help you with something?"

Amena tried her best to sound official. "No ma'am, I just had a few quick questions which I hope you can answer." Amena was impressed with herself.

The lady agreed and sent the young child inside the house. "Sure, I would be happy to help you out. What would you like to know?" She asked.

Amena asked if she knew the gentleman, whether or not she had seen or knew Aasha, as well as a few questions about the gentleman's demeanour. The lady seemed to be very knowledgeable about the gentleman and had even met Aasha a couple of times socially.

The lady explained that she even had dated the gentleman at one time years ago. They had broken up over his extreme jealousy. Apparently, he became irate if he even suspected her of talking to another man. This scared the lady and after he hit her over it once, she broke up with him.

Eventually, they became friends again. The lady said she assumed that he'd learned a lesson but had noticed a few times when he seemed very controlling over Aasha. She had heard from others in the neighbourhood that they argued regularly. No one had said much else to her. Generally, people keep to themselves there. "They don't pry," she said.

Amena got the impression that there was more to this story. She wondered if she would get anything from her family and friends. She remembered where Aasha used to live and drove to her mother's home.

Aasha's mother was home. Amena could tell she had been crying all night when she answered the door. She recognized Amena immediately and gave her a warm hug. Amena explained why she was there and offered her condolences. They sat down and talked about the old days for a few hours. Aasha's mom explained that she had numerous concerns about the relationship because she had seen her daughter with multiple bruises time after time. Aasha always had a poor excuse for the bruising.

This information worried Amena and she thought about telling this to her friend from the law enforcement, who had helped her with the files. It was wonderful seeing Aasha's mom again, although the circumstances which had made them meet again were gruesome. Amena made her way back to the police station. Although they were not happy that Amena had been probing and sniffing around on her own, they were happy to receive the information for their files.

She was told that forensics just sent their report in and the fingerprints on the murder weapon did belong to Aasha's former boyfriend. They had also found an eyewitness that placed him at the scene at the time of the murder and went against his earlier plea of alibi.

Amena found out later that the police had arrested and charged the ex-boyfriend with murdering Aasha after they caught him trying to leave town. Amena was relieved. After the police took her statement, Amena went home, satisfied that she did the best she could for her friend.

Eventually, the case went to trial and the ex-boyfriend was found guilty of murdering Aasha. His motive? "She was too happy. She had the audacity to be happy without me," he laughed. He was labelled a killer with psychopathic tendencies and the case was closed. Now every class reunion, the class members get together and run a special campaign against domestic abuse in memory of their friend Aasha.

18

THE ACCIDENTAL DICTATOR

by Karthik C.

P rofessor Sahil Butt adjusted his tortoise-shell glasses on his sharp nose as he took out a folded kerchief from his brown pant pocket. He caressed the little box inside before pulling out the piece of cloth and holding it to his nose. He took a chalk from the box near the lectern and broke it into two before writing 'free speech' on the already scribbled blackboard. He dropped a piece of chalk while palming the other. He put his kerchief back in his pocket and again ran a finger on the smooth box inside before turning to his students.

"This is the essence of any society. The basic right. If a civilization has to function, then its citizens must be able to think and speak their minds. There is a clear consensus on this from philosophers to historians; everyone agrees that freedom of expression is the soul of every constitution, the very heart of a healthy democracy. If we retrospect, every major downfall of nations and the rise of various revolutions can be attributed to this fundamental right – be it by either curbing it or downright abolishing it. Forgetting freedom of speech is a slippery slope into fascism. It was like John Milton said: "Give me the liberty to know, to utter, and to argue freely according to conscience, above all liberties." Freedom of speech gives you an identity which becomes your ideology. Simply put, if there is no freedom of speech, there is no identity, period. Any questions?" asked Sahil, pausing. "All right. Have a nice weekend. I will meet you all on Monday."

Sahil Butt kept rolling the chalk in one hand, with the other holding the box tightly inside his pocket as he looked at the slow exodus of his students. He had waited a long time for this moment, but he was filled with apprehension, nonetheless. It was time to exercise his right of expression. This day would change his life forever.

***

The lights were dim, and so was the murmur of conversation throughout the little restaurant. There was a slight hum from the large television screen where a 24x7 news channel was running. The small booths were placed right in front of the screen, opposite the doorway, with the kitchen and restrooms on either side of them.

The focused light from the low-hanging bulb was dull but warm, giving each table a feel of its own. It was as if each booth was draped by an invisible blanket, giving its inhabitants the illusion of privacy and the comfort of home.

"Ever since I was a child, I have dreaded one thing: loneliness. I have seen many suffer from its grasp. I have seen them grow old with no one else around them, having solitary meals with nothing but the television for their company. All my life, I've strived to fit into a mould. I have always been alone, but now, I seek your companionship. Jessica Praxton, will you cure my loneliness? Will you be my friend, my wife, my eternal travel partner throughout life?" Sahil Butt was holding out a ring in his right hand as he sat across his girlfriend in the corner booth of their favourite café. The little box was now lying empty on the table, beside the unopened menu.

Jessica Praxton gazed at Sahil with her small but bright eyes. She actually had to bend down to meet his gaze. She did it very subtly as she was used to it by now. It had been an uncomfortable topic to discuss, her being an inch and a half taller than him, especially when they began to date. She did make sure to make him as comfortable as possible. She found Sahil to be a very delicate being, an introvert with little to no social activities. She had very little knowledge about his upbringing, but she loved him for his old-school charm, his mild-mannered etiquette and humility, his liberal ideologies, and most importantly, his empathy. She cared less about his unknown past or his short stature, and more about the man with a big heart who was moulding future generations. And now, she would be caring about her future husband. And a bit more, apparently.

Sahil looked at the bright eyes and could see that the corners were pooling up. His heart was beating hard against his chest all the way from his university to the café, but the mere sight of Jessica had soothed his jitters. Her perpetual smile appeared to communicate with his heart just like a mother to her child, caressing it, saying that everything would be all right, that he was safe. It was this comfort that he had been deprived of ever since he was a child.

He had run away from his family to find solace in strange lands. He had given up hopes of ever finding it and couldn't believe his luck when he finally found his saving grace, his guardian angel. "Yes, I will," said Jessica, and Sahil smiled the widest smile that she had ever seen as he slipped the ring through her finger. She couldn't believe the timing.

"I do, Sahil. I do accept you as my future husband – and the father of my child."

Sahil gasped and gaped at Jessica, who nodded as she caressed her tummy.

"I swear that I would never let any harm befall you, or my child. I will love you both till my last breath. But when did you come to know? I thought I was the one with a surprise. Tell me everything," Sahil gushed, saying everything at once.

"I will. But first, allow me to use the washroom," Jessica replied as she excused herself, grinning like a little girl.

Sahil looked at her go and saw a few people huddled near the television, murmuring excitedly. He craned his neck to get a better view, and then suddenly stood up and walked briskly to the screen, palming the empty ring box. The anchor was reporting a piece of breaking news as feeds from different cameras overlapped each other on the screen.

'Zuber Tihani, the first-born son of the President of the Republic of Zana, has been killed. Early reports seem to indicate that he was assassinated inside the Mauritius International Airport. His body was recovered from the restroom with puncture marks between his toes. The cause of death is ideated to be poisoning. There have been no claims on the hit so far. Speculations are rife that this might be a retaliatory attack after the nation's announcement of enriching weapons' grade uranium and warning its neighbours of definite and decisive action by the aging President Suleiman Tihani. Many analysts considered the deceased Zuber Tihani to be the heir apparent, and this event might trigger a power vacuum. Zuber Tihani, like his father, was a conservative hardliner and wanted absolute hegemony in the corrosive middle east. The NATO considers Suleiman Tihani to be a warmonger and a dictator, and there have been alleged unsuccessful covert operations by the USA to overthrow the fascist regime...'

Just as Sahil and others around him started to grasp what was happening, three sturdy men in masks entered the café. One of them held the door open, not allowing anyone to enter or exit. He held a Kalashnikov in his hand. There were muffled screams and a sense of uncertainty as realisation dawned on the late evening patrons.

One of the men quickly masked Sahil with a black bag and the other injected a turbid liquid into his neck. Within fifteen seconds, Sahil was transferred into a nondescript black SUV with tinted windows which soon disappeared into the twilight traffic. All that remained of Sahil for Jessica Praxton, who had just come out of the restroom, was the ring, which now seemed to have lost its lustre.

***

The room was piercingly bright. The added smell of saturated ammonia felt nauseating. There was complete silence apart from the miscellaneous beeps from myriad instruments. It was in sharp contrast with the outside of the hospice where thousands and thousands of people had taken to the streets, either mourning their young leader or praying for the recovery of their President.

Sahil Butt sat, reclining at the back, as he rolled the empty ring box absent-mindedly, with a cloth to cover his sensitive nose. Six five-star generals surrounded the bed on which the President of the Republic of Zana now lay. Slowly, all of them left, murmuring their wishes to Sahil.

With a delicate wave, Suleiman Tihani, the dreaded dictator, signalled his youngest and now his only living heir, Sahil Tihani to tend to him. He had been hospitalized because of an apparent heart attack as soon as he had heard the news of his eldest son's unexpected demise.

"Son, it's time. What have you decided?" Suleiman asked, his hand resting on Sahil's.

"I – I don't know, Father. You know I cannot," said Sahil.

"Communism is so pure that it is inherently flawed. For you to implement it, you need to be a fascist," said Suleiman. "Hoping that it must come naturally to everyone is a fool's pipe dream. We have been watching you. I understand your turmoil. But I need you. The country needs you. Do not go by the western propaganda. They are trying to sully us in the eyes of the world. They have our ignorant neighbour in their pockets. They are pushing us to make the first move so that NATO can have Casus belli to obliterate us. Zuber, unfortunately, fell prey to that.

"We are now secluded, but not helpless. We can soon produce nuclear weapons, our deterrent. All this is because of the news of the discovery of the oil wells. I know that one of my generals leaked that to the west," he sighed, dejectedly, shaking his head. "They are vultures circling above me. I fear a mutiny, a coup. They will welcome war or sell our resources to the west. We are slowly becoming self-sufficient. You have seen the reports; our economy is booming despite many sanctions and illegal embargos.

"The quality of life has never been better. Isolation is required to ward off hyenas. It's a hibernating cocoon from which we will fly. I hope you understand what is required. I know it's a sacrifice. I did not want any of this for you, neither did your mother or Zuber, but now, thirty-three million citizens need you. Save us, son. Help us fly," said Suleiman, "and remember, no loose ends." Sahil placed his hand on Suleiman's wrinkled knuckles, and a small teardrop fell, taking away with it his dreams and promises.

***

The enormous television screen was dwarfed in comparison to the huge dining room. The journalist was reporting the morning news as other esteemed panellists waited to debate on it.

'It was the last day of the three-month mourning of Suleiman Tihani and his son Zuber Tihani. In a surprising turn of events for the small nation, the absentee son, Sahil Tihani, appeared and staked claim without protest as the new President. The new leadership did not change the past narrative. Whilst at a lavish military parade, which was organized as a statement to the west, the Supreme Leader stated his hatred towards capitalism, and vowed to avenge his brother's demise, and called for death to the west. He was well-received by his country's citizens…'

The lavish oak table stretched along the long hall of the dining room, where the new President of the Republic of Zana, Sahil Tihani, sat alone, having his breakfast and looking at the television blankly. Beside his elaborate tableware were expunged records of his past life, and a report with his signature, sanctioning the death of one Ms. Jessica Praxton and her unborn child. The small, ring-less box sat on top of it.

19

THE LAST WISH

by Deepshikha Saw

It was eleven in the morning. I was in the office when my phone rang. Answering it, I took a look around at the people, making sure I was in view. After a while, my hands started to tremble, and I gasped in shock. I couldn't stand still. My heartbeats got faster, and panic rushed through my veins.

I hailed a cab and reached the crime scene. My fiancé had been murdered! On my way to his apartment, I kept staring at my ring, which was his only memory left with me. I reached the building to find cops gathered around and a crowd of by-standers blocking the way. I stepped out of the car, suddenly aware of countless pairs of eyes on me. I saw his family grieving near his body, which lay on a stretcher near the ambulance. Show-offs, I thought nastily.

No one was allowed near the crime scene, but I was called in for interrogation by the police officers. He lived on the fourth floor of the building, where he was killed. I heard the cops asking for his body to be taken away for autopsy, and one of them mentioned that there were no bloodstains on his body. It majorly pointed to murder by asphyxiation, as there were no other marks or injuries to be found. My body went rigid after listening to that.

My mind numb, I somehow managed to enter the now topsy-turvy apartment, where the cops had recreated the scene and were looking for evidence. Calling me aside, a female cop interrogated me. I was nervous and started to perspire but held on to my sanity for dear life. I cooperated with the cops and even asked them to interrogate the neighbours. "Time of death?" The inspector asked an officer. "It was around eight in the morning, sir. The body was on the floor when the servant forcefully opened the door," the officer replied. They questioned where I was during those hours.

"I was in my office since eight in the morning. I woke up early today, and during that time, I was at home with my family," I replied with utmost confidence.

"On a Saturday?" He asked and I tensed.

"Yes, I had some extra work to complete and had to go to the office," I stuttered. He stared at me for a couple of seconds and then turned back to his officers and continued to investigate. Everyone around had a gloomy face while people who knew him couldn't stop crying. Only I knew how pure he was as a person.

I started feeling uneasy, guilt creeping up inside. I was sobbing when his mother came to me all teary-eyed. "I am sorry, child" she wailed. Just as one of the officers was within earshot, I finally showed some courage and asked her where she was. With a pause, she said that she was with her husband at their apartment when they heard the news.

"Didn't you mostly spend your weekends with him? It's so strange that he was killed on the one weekend you didn't visit him," I said, loud enough for the officer to hear. I could feel I briefly had his attention. After all, it was possible. She and her husband, to whom she was married after my fiancé's real father had died, had always been greedy for his property.

Just then, his sister arrived, another drama queen. She was dressed in white and had a tear-stricken face, and was accompanied by her husband. I never liked that woman. She was always fishy and annoyingly melodramatic. She came crying to me and hugged me with her eyes filled with crocodile tears.

The way she behaved was just so strange. After the post-mortem of his body, we went to the funeral, where I saw him one last time. His sister shouted, "I wish I was there for you, brother!" As if she actually cared! She had always been jealous of him. After all, he had more money than her alcoholic husband.

Since I knew them for more than five years, I knew she had never really shown up when he needed her. I was the one taking care of him. None of the family members seemed keen to question the cops' progress or answer their questions. I had always felt something was oddly wrong between them.

I decided to contact the police about it. "The family is involved!" I whispered to the chief inspector at the funeral. His reaction was strange. He said sternly, "You are all suspects. It'd be better for you to not give judgments." I immediately kept quiet.

"Oh my god! Why did this have to happen?" shouted Samuel, his best friend. He came in his black Mercedes as usual. Hugging the coffin, he then hugged his mother, his sister and then finally came to me. I turned on my relentless crying, and he hugged me and consoled me.

I asked him where he was and how he got the news. He replied that he was in his apartment with his girlfriend when his phone rang. He rushed down to say goodbye for one last time to his beloved friend.

"Didn't you fight with her?" I asked him innocently, to which he replied that everything had been sorted out in the past two days. I still couldn't come to terms with what he'd said. He always had problems with his girlfriend, and that was a major reason behind him being jealous of our happy relationship. I wondered how everything had suddenly worked out between them.

After interrogating us again, the police sent us home and asked us to come again the next day. I reached home in a hurry and took a shower. I couldn't stop thinking about him. All the memories of him kept floating in my mind. Guilt was building up inside me, yet, at the same time, I couldn't help but feel lighter.

I deleted my pictures with him on my phone. I couldn't bear to see his face. My life had turned upside down, everything had fallen apart, and I had no idea how this was going to end. I was feeling anxious and getting panic attacks. I was all alone at my apartment, and the familiar pang of loneliness struck again.

I knew I had to go for the interrogation the next day. I couldn't risk coming off as even a little suspicious. I was nervous, but I knew I could handle it. I had to lie again and again unless the case got closed. I had to pretend for a longer time. Whom could I try to keep pinning it on? Who had a stronger motive? The mother? Or the sister? Or the friend? I had to come up with some plan or the other. The entire family could rot in hell for all I cared.

My mind reeling with possibilities, I then took out the gloves from the garbage to burn them as I couldn't risk leaving any evidence behind. The cops would definitely come by to check my house. I could picture my gloved hands around his throat, as I crushed his Adam's apple, staring into his eyes as the colour in them drained away. I didn't expect that things would turn out this way, but I had the confidence to manipulate them, I kept reminding myself.

I thought back to that day. As much I would miss him, the bastard deserved what was coming for him. He was cheating on me, for God's sake! The relationship had become so toxic. So, I carried out my wish, killing him while he was asleep. The only task which had been hard was to escape from the building. Also, shifting his body to the floor hadn't been easy either. Reminiscing the events, I finally took my sleeping pills.

20

LA ATRACO

by Prajwal Shukla

I was waiting in the runaway car for my boys while they robbed a bank. Soon enough, I'd get them to safety and then split ways. The engine was up and running and my reflexes, high. It was an in-and-out job, with no body count. But annoyingly, we had to switch to Plan B.

Now, Plan B was that they'd dress as hostages if the cops were called, and some wannabe hero did call them. They ran out with other hostages from the back door with all the bags of money having been pushed down the drains. I rushed to the drop-off. Our Russian friends were waiting down with a net to catch the bags at the first turn the drain made.

When we reached, Vradkik said they got the bags out and dumped them in their van but the driver escaped with the bags. Furious, we chased him. The driver had ditched the van at a dumpster and had gotten into a garbage truck. But we were at his tail, and soon enough, caught him. Vradkik, furious, filled his guts with lead, with a finishing touch on his temple.

We split the money and resumed our lives, until yesterday, when Vradkik sent an emergency distress signal. His mates were dead. We were all being hunted one after the other by the getaway driver's brother, Potchinki. We even regrouped, but to no avail. Vradkik died, too.

We plotted a plan to trap Potchinki by calling him out to one of us as bait. Six of us against one. Now, we didn't know we had a mole amongst us. On D-Day, when we reached the decided place, we were gassed and knocked out. We woke up tied to chairs, six feet away from each other; a bomb in the centre of the semi-circle and a screen in front of us. A pre-recorded message said, "*Paga tu deuda.* (Pay your debt.)"

We couldn't all leave. One of us had to stay back to keep the bomb from exploding, and that person had the key on them. We tried to search for it, and the key fell out of my pocket. I knew that this was it. But Boldon threw himself on the bomb, giving us the time to escape. I couldn't save him. I couldn't save my friend.

But it wasn't over. It was time to attack. We vowed to bring down Potchinki. We found out how he knew about the gathering and from where he got his bomb. We split up but stayed connected. Evidence from the blast suggested it was illegally assembled with explosive material that was only available in Istanbul. Unfortunately, the trip to Istanbul was fruitless. The dealer had no clue which buyer it could be. Potchinki had covered his tracks well.

Fortunately, we had a copy of the recorded message he sent us, and we found where the stream came from. It was at an outpost near Togo, in Central Africa. We found a team of underground hackers and coders who ran illegal businesses on the deep web. They wouldn't speak unless we made them an irrefutable offer. With a little bribing and bargaining, we got ourselves a lead.

The call was made from Potchinki's old residence in South America, a safe house in Rio. We suspected we might hit another dead-end. Before going to Rio, Badland from the ground team managed to get his hands on the hidden surveillance footage from the camera that he had installed for security a day before we met. Potchinki didn't know this. We saw the masked maniac set up the trap that we walked into.

On our way from the airport in Rio, we saw a van passing us by. The painting on the side of the van looked eerily familiar. It belonged to Badland's cousin who had helped us with the nets. The bumper sticker and a quick run on the plates confirmed this information. We turned around and followed it. Badland wasn't responding and it wasn't a good sign. We ended up tailing the van to a secluded housing area. A dog handler was returning a rescue dog. We split up. Ramon and I continued tracking the van and the rest went in search of Badland.

We decided to meet Potchinki and negotiate. As we followed the van, it reached the edge of a cliff and stopped. Puzzled, we walked towards it. The driver had his back to us, but all he said was, *"Paga tu deuda."* A second later, we got hit on our heads from behind.

We woke up with our faces masked and wrists tied to some sort of pipes in a damp and moist place. I could hear water dripping. Assuming that Ramon was tied up along with me in the same room, I tried to call out to him with every bit of energy left in my body. Soft rays of sunlight were brushing against me. They were slight and concentrated, so I assumed they were coming from a partially open window. I called out to Ramon a few more times before giving up.

My head was throbbing, and my body was giving up. I felt light-headed and extremely weak. A few minutes later, I heard noises. Someone had a knife and just then, I heard shouts from not far away. The next moment, my wrists were free as I fell onto a shoulder. It was Ramon. "I've got you," he said, "come on. Let's get out of here."

We came across a cheap fence that surrounded the area and jumped over it. Locating the nearest fuel station, we called our team. We laid low till we made progress in finding Potchinki.

They arranged to meet at a warehouse 20 miles from our location. Ramon and I found a motel to stay at until the situation was safe, and we could move out. But I insisted we go to the warehouse immediately and look for Badland. "Trust the team," Ramon insisted confidently. The drugs had rendered me weak and I was starving. Ordering dinner, we settled in and called it a day.

At dawn, I sneaked out to the warehouse. I hitchhiked on a car and asked to be dropped off at the location. Ramon was still asleep. Once at the warehouse, I began looking for Badland. After an hour of futile searching, I began to fear he was dead. Just then, I found him tied up and abandoned in a secluded part of the place. I tried to wake him up, but he was knocked out.

I scanned the area to find something to untie him. Unfortunately, I wasn't alone. I heard a gun cock. Taking shallow breaths and trying my best not to show my anxiety on my face, I turned around to face the guest, only to be left open-mouthed and dumb founded.

"Boldon?" I said, too shocked to move.

"I'm sorry, I really am," he said. "I had no choice. He threatened to kill my family."

Rage boiled inside me. But I couldn't afford to be impulsive. I had underestimated Potchinki. I tried to keep Boldon wrapped up in conversation.

"So that's why you have Badland. You are the masked man."

"Yes." He sounded impatient.

"Why not kill him?"

"I couldn't do it. Not to him. Not… Not Badland."

While Boldon talked, I saw a shadow of a figure sneaking up behind him. Within the split of a second, I heard a gunshot and Boldon fell down. Blood pooled around his leg.

"Ramon," Boldon gasped as he faced the shooter and fell to the ground, clutching his foot in pain.

"I told you to stay put," Ramon said to me sternly.

Suddenly, we were blinded by an excruciating white light from overhead spotlights. Before we could figure out what was going on, a voice boomed, "Welcome, rats in a trap." It was Potchinki. The next second, gunshots started going off from all sides.

We were outnumbered. Not losing hope, we managed to kill some of his people despite the lack of vision. Soon enough, the rest of our men came to our rescue. Together, we managed to kill all his goons and finally capture him. We offered him half the stolen money.

He scoffed. "Do you think I did this for money?"

We all looked at each other, unsure how to answer.

"You killed my brother," He bellowed.

"It wasn't us!" I snapped. "The Russians did it. Your brother had an arrangement with us, and he didn't keep his end of the deal."

"Either way, you have to pay. Not to me, but to him."

"Him?"

"You fools kept thinking I was the threat." He chuckled manically.

Before he could laugh any more, I knocked out some of his teeth. "You better start talking," I seethed.

"He's coming."

"Who's coming?" I shouted.

"El Diablo."

There was dead silence.

"El Diablo. One of the seven drug lords ruling the crime scene of the world - the name which terrorises the deadliest of the deadly. One of the masterminds behind The Magician's Cape, and my father." He sneered.

I stared at him dumbly, unable to breathe. That was when it hit me how deeply sunk we were. I'd prefer being sentenced for years.

Just then, we heard the churning of gravel and looked out the warehouse to see five Range Rovers stop near us. An army of men in black stepped out from the cars except one. The door of the last car opened, and a single man stepped out.

Followed by his men, he started walking towards us, his eyes never leaving mine. My throat went dry.

"What gives you the right to tie my son up like that?" El Diablo snarled.

Realizing he was speaking to me, I cleared my throat.

"Mr. Diablo, sir, we don't want any hassle. He tried to avenge his brother's death but we're not his killers. There was a heist. Your son didn't make it."

"And what makes you think you did?"

"I'm deeply sorry for your loss." I wasn't. "We're willing to make up for it."

"My son was murdered." He growled.

"Yes, because the idiot tried to run off with money that was rightfully ours." I snapped. Ramon gave me a look. No one snapped at El Diablo.

Annoyed, El Diablo kicked at a pebble. "I always wanted my son to take over my business. But the fool wanted to start on his own. Look where it got him. If you want to clean this mess, you'll prove your worth to me. All of you. If even one of you tries to mess around, I'll pull the reins on your lives."

"How do we do that, sir?"

"Work for me."

It seemed an offer that would keep us alive. We all nodded.

"Finally, some sensible ones. For your safety, you'll each go alone with one of my men to a safe house where you'll be kept until further instructions. Your faces will be covered. You are not to see anything besides your workplace."

Something was fishy, but I let it go. Covering each of our faces from head to neck, we were all taken in different cars. Half an hour later, we screeched to a stop. I wondered what was wrong.

The car door opened, and I was manhandled by a firm grip of hands. My hands were pinned behind me, and I didn't dare ask. A cold breeze gushed against me. The mask was yanked off my face, and what I saw shook me to the bones.

I was standing at the edge of a cliff, and a huge, tall man flung me over with my feet dangling. "Boss's orders," he shrugged.

As loudly and clearly as I could, I yelled, "No! I will, I will... *Paga... Pagaré... Mi. deuda... Pagaré Mi Deuda... por favor.*"

"Boss will be pleased to have you serve him," he said, then spoke into the radio, "He passed."

21

I AM MICHELLE

by Santhosh Ganesan

Prologue: Present Day

The wind blows softly where my story begins. But in Southfield, people are always faster than the wind – hustling with hectic work schedules. Consequently, they don't have enough time to check their surroundings. Maybe that is why they hold a deep, dark secret that is known only to them. But I am here to tell you mine.

I'm Michelle Wheeler, a 26-year-old woman of passion and discipline. After practicing 3D visual art for almost seven years of my life, I was finally hired as a professional at the V Architect Studio. I had done tons of internships before, but no one seemed to want me in their workplace. Maybe I was too raw in what I did, or maybe people got jobs by getting in their employers' beds. This was a pretty normal thing that happened here in Southfield, so I wasn't surprised when that high school bitch Roxanne got hired in just one meeting.

The work environment used to be pretty good. But tons of faces frowning with vengeance roamed around my cubicle. It had been the same old story for the last 2 years of my life. I didn't blame them, though. I was good at my job. And I remained in good books with the CEO, Margaret. She was a bloodsucker for all – harsh, rude, and direct. But considering her past, one could understand. She was a self-made businesswoman who had picked herself up off the streets, worked as a prison guard, studied technology on her own, and founded the V studio. Once, she yelled at an employee so bad he almost drove himself into depression and became suicidal.

But that never happened to me. I had closed 170 Projects in a quarter while my peers struggled to achieve the target of just 100. All VIP clients were always handed over to me since I always kept my promise, time and quality-wise. It added up to the hatred my peers had towards me, but what was I to do? I couldn't compromise just so I could get on good terms with them. Amanda hated me the most, and the feeling was mutual.

But Lucy was different. She always had my back no matter what. She had a rough history, too, but she had no choice when she was forced to work with the dark web under pressure. She was a bold, brave woman who feared nobody because she had already seen the worst. And she was never embarrassed to approach me for help. She looked up to me as her mentor, and to me, she was my best friend.

Presently, the time is 11:30 p.m. No one is on the streets. I draw out my lighter and light it up. "Let's see some action baby," I whisper into the dark and drop my lighter. Half an hour from now, this place and two people will be nothing but just ashes.

***

Three days earlier

"Michelle! In my office! Now!" Margret roared. My face turned pale. I could hear my colleagues snicker. Random whispers immediately filled the room: 'Bitch is getting it today', 'Nobody can stay Queen too long', and 'I bet you 10 bucks she'll come out sobbing'. I shrugged the voices off and followed Margret in.

"Yes, Margret. Is everything alright?"

"You tell me!" She thundered.

"But I –" I stammered, staring at her, my mind blank.

"Remember GNB's big project Amanda was working on?"

"Amanda? No, I was working on that one. I even built a blue pr–"

She cut me off, "Do I look like a fool, Michelle? Amanda was standing right here a few days ago when she presented her plan," she yelled, lighting up her cigarette. 'No smoking' was written all over our cubicles, but you couldn't see into Margret's cabin only because of the smoke left behind half a dozen cigarettes which she smoked every day.

"You stole her project and sold it to the Spark Studio! Why would you do that?" Exactly. Why would I do that? Spark was V Architect's sworn enemy.

"You have to believe me, Margaret. I didn't do it. The papers are on my desk. Please, let me prove it to you," I said, and after contemplating a little, she nodded.

I quickly sprinted to my desk and pulled out my drawer. Where the heck was it? Realization dawned. Amanda must've stolen it and sold it to them. But why would she do that? She hated me, but I never imagined she would want to sabotage my career. Just as I looked up and turned around, Margret was standing in front of me, her cigar lit in one hand.

"Found it, darling?" My hands went cold. "How would you? It is right here," she said, holding out a rolled white chart.

"Yes! That's it. That's what I've been working on."

"This is Amanda's. You stole this, made copies of it on my printer, and sold it to your boyfriend, you whore. David just shared the finished video of your blueprint on the tool and it has caught everyone's attention," she bellowed. She just called me a whore in front of the entire office.

"I didn't steal it, Margret, that plan is mine. I'm sure someone stole it from me, sold it, and framed me. I can tell you every detail about it. And David and I aren't even together anymore," my voice trailed off.

David was an ex-employee and manager at the V studio. He was the one who helped me get a job here. We were in love for almost three years before he decided to leave. It wasn't entirely his fault. I was too harsh on him and I did a couple of regrettable things. Once, I broke into his house and ruined all his expensive shirts because he liked a half-naked girl's photo on Instagram.

"You're fired, Michelle. I want you to out of my office. Now. I need no traitors here, or I'll report this and have you blacklisted." She stomped off. The entire floor didn't expect this. Sure, they thought I'd get yelled at or be thrown a couple of swear-words, but this was not what they imagined. Neither did I. Lucy walked towards me and held my hand.

"I know you didn't do this, Michelle," she whispered. I walked back to my desk, trying to hold all my tears back, and gathered all my things. Amanda. *That bitch.*

***

It was 4 a.m. and I hadn't even blinked. I spent the last two days in my room. I just couldn't come to terms with the fact that I was fired for something I didn't even do. My mind went into overdrive and I had only one name circling around in my mind – Amanda. I put my phone on the bed and pulled up my blanket. Two years – I invested two years in V Studio and she mercilessly kicked me out in front of the entire office. She humiliated me and didn't even bother to hear me out – all this for the countless, sleepless nights and overtime working days at work. I knew what I had to do. I picked up my phone and texted Lucy.

Me: Hey

Lucy: Not able to sleep?

Me: No. You up too?

Lucy: I was reading a book and lost track of time.

Me: Hmm.

Lucy: Hmm?

Me: Can you come over? I need to talk.

Lucy: Now? Sure. I'll be there in fifteen.

Me: Don't knock. Bring your spare key and come upstairs.

Lucy: Roger that. Over.

I giggled and got up to go the bathroom. By the time I came out, Lucy was already in my bed, half-naked.

"Whoa!"

"What! You asked me to come and you disappear?" she said, taking off her bra.

"I had to pee," I said, and held my breath. She was hot!

"What happened?"

"I texted David."

"What? Did you ask him to come too?" She asked, winking her eyes at me. That would be steamier, I thought in my head.

"I did, but not now. We'll meet him at the office tomorrow, 11 p.m."

"You mean tonight? But it's Saturday. Nobody will be there."

"Amanda will. I overheard her tell Margret that she would be working the nightshift for the weekend."

"Why did you call me now?" She ran her hands up and down my thigh.

"I need you to do me a favour." Lucy had a history of hacking. I took off my bra and pushed my breasts in her face.

"Can you help me block the phone lines of the office until midnight, darling?" She paused for a while. Her hands stroked around my chest and pinched my nipples.

"Uh okay, it'll take a couple of hours to shut it down, but why?"

"I don't need disturbance when I talk to them." We kiss passionately.

In minutes, she was under me and I made her breathless. When we were done, she fell asleep in an instant while I stayed wide awake. This had to be planned well.

***

Epilogue: Ashes

I haven't slept, but I feel like I'm filled with energy – the energy of vengeance. Adrenaline gushes through my veins. It feels like it's the longest day of my life. Lucy spent the night at my place and worked on tapping the phone lines as soon as she woke up. That night was the most silent night that I had ever witnessed. But what's about to happen in the middle of this nothingness will shake up the entire city.

Amanda is sitting at her desk. I watch her click on her laptop. I walk in and she looks at me with surprise. She asks me why I'm here, and by then, David has already walked in the room. Lucy is outside in her car, keeping an eye on the street. It's around 10 p.m. and the entire city is asleep. I turn to David and my jaw almost drops. He looks incredible. That swine.

"Tell me why you did it," I say and sink in the chair in front of them.

"Did what? Why did you call us?" David asks and I grin.

"Amanda was already here."

"Michelle... Oh my god, is this about the blueprints?" he sighs.

"Aha," I say triumphantly and walk closer to her chair. She picks up the landline and dials in.

"Oh, baby, you think I'd come unprepared? All lines are tapped."

David gets up, trying to tackle me. I take out my brass knuckles.

"David, sit down before I break your face."

Carefully sitting down, David then confesses that it was all his idea. He tells me how he tricked Amanda into bringing a parcel to his office that was tipped off by Margret herself. I couldn't believe my ears.

"We fell in love, Michelle. She hated you. We staged this ever since," David says. I feel the blood rushing to my face. There's not much time. I immediately rush out Amanda and lock David in his cabin. Amanda immediately apologises and agrees to help me.

"I'm burning this place down," I say. She's nervous at first, but I assure her, if she keeps quiet and follows the plan, nobody would suspect her. All that hatred against Margret works to my advantage. She pings Margret and calls her to the office, saying it's an emergency. We wait for her, and the moment she walks in, we take the back exit. I tell Amanda to leave immediately.

It's Endgame, whore.

***

Reporter on TV: *The V architect studio burned and collapsed by midnight. We are yet to find out how the office caught fire. Amanda, an employee, says she sensed a burning smell and ran out of the office immediately. The CEO and her affair were in the Cabin when she went in to warn them. Sadly, they did not make it out alive.*

Keep watching Southfield Times for more updates.

22

AN IMMINENT MURDER

by Deepshikha Saw

Walking down the gate, I hurried to the bus station. I had to solve an important case and I couldn't back off now.

While riding the bus, I took out my cigar and took a drag. Cigars were miraculous stress busters for me. If you were living in the '80s, you'd know how famous the brown suitcases were back then. Being a detective, it was my old friend.

I reached the town for my new case. I decided to walk as it was just a few blocks away. When I reached the place, the sight of a huge palace-like structure blew my mind. I had never heard about it in the upstate. I was surprised by such a beautiful piece of architecture that looked like heaven on Earth. A beautiful lady opened the door. She had a really pretty face, a bedazzling smile with dimples and sparkling green eyes, wearing a simple yet pretty pink gown. She smiled at me and asked, "How may I help you, sir?"

I was taken aback by the question, given the circumstances under which I had been called. "I am Mr. Ronert Gabriel, the detective tasked to solve the murder case of Mr. David. May I talk to Miss Nova?" I introduced myself.

She looked me in the eye, and with a gracious smile, asked me to follow her. "This way, sir. Madam might be resting for now." I followed her to the third floor, where there was a huge room with mystical paintings on the wall with brownish texture all over. I saw Miss Nova lying on the bed, her long brown hair falling around her face and down to her shoulders, her pale skin making her look like a porcelain doll. The lady gently woke her up, carefully sitting her up in bed. There was something odd in the way she regarded Miss Nova. Smiling at me, Miss Nova politely asked the lady to leave.

"Hello, Mr. Ronert, I really appreciate you coming here," she said.

"Miss Nova, I need to ask you a few questions about the murder," I replied.

As if on cue, she broke down and replied, "I could never forgive the person who killed him!" I had my suspicions pinned on a family member. Somehow, the environment and the eerie coolness in the air despite a murder having taken place put things under that spotlight more than anything.

"Who else lives here with you, Miss Nova?" I asked her.

"It was just my grandfather and I. After my parents died, he was the one who raised me. I was about to get married but it was called off after this unfortunate incident." She kept sobbing.

"Why was your wedding put off and not postponed?" I asked curiously.

"My fiancé didn't want to get married to me after such a morbid incident. He thought it was a bad omen." What a bundle of nonsense, I thought. Reminding myself that I had a murder case at hand, I let that slide.

"I need to know what exactly happened, Miss Nova. How were things before you found him?" I asked her in a soft tone.

She took some time, started weeping again, and said, "I was in my room. Rosy was downstairs cleaning our guest room when we heard the scream and ran towards his room." After brushing aside her tears, she continued, "We saw him lying on the floor with blood all over his body, with a knife lying around him."

"A knife," I repeated, taking notes. "Did the cops find any leads?"

"I'm not sure what they found, but they took the knife away for fingerprints. I don't think they found anything on it either," she replied with sudden confidence in her tone.

"They didn't find any fingerprints on the knife? Did they take samples of your fingerprints? Or Rosy's?"

I could see her getting all jittery. She frowned before answering, "I don't know about it. It was their job; I just wish I could get my grandfather back!" And she started crying again. This time, I felt more annoyed at her than sympathetic. Her story just didn't seem believable. I needed to know the truth. Rosy was not far away, rather just standing outside the room, trying to eavesdrop.

"I'd like to talk to Rosy as well."

"Yes, although I don't think she has done anything." She laughed trying but failing to sound genuine.

I could see, she was really scared. Rosy was standing just outside the room, and upon seeing me coming, she pretended to clean the flower vase. "Ms. Rosy, I would like to ask you a few questions, if you can co-operate with me?" I asked softly.

She looked down for a few seconds before replying with a smile, "Yes sir, I can answer all your questions."

"Where were you when Mr. David was killed?" I asked.

"I was downstairs, cleaning the guest room, as madam asked me to. When I heard his scream, I ran to the third floor, where I saw him lying down on the floor." After a short pause, she continued, "I also saw a knife on the floor, and he was covered with blood all over his body."

I took out my cigar. Something felt amiss. Miss Nova was not clear about what happened to the knife, and Ms. Rosy's alibi seemed practiced. They both had the same narrative; could it have been doubly planned?

Miss Nova would have gotten his property anyway. Why would she kill him? And why would Rosy help her? I kept asking myself. As I turned back to go back downstairs, I had a clear view into Miss Nova's bedroom where Rosy was back at her bedside, tucking her in bed. I couldn't help but feel strange. And then, out of nowhere, it hit me. Of course! The way Rosy woke Miss Nova up, the way she gazed at her, the way Rosy's hands lingered just a little longer as she woke Miss Nova up – *They were in love!*

The renowned and reputed Mr. David finding out about his granddaughter's secret affair with a female, and that too with the housekeeper no less, could not have been a pleasant scene. It would stain his image in more ways than one if society found out. Of course he would be against it.

I started walking towards the room where Mr. David had been killed, wanting to find out more. I got the uneasy feeling of someone walking up behind me. I turned around to see, but there was no one. Suddenly, something pierced my back, and the pain began to seep through agonizingly. It took me a while to realise the stab of a knife.

My vision started to blur, and I gasped, struggling to breathe amidst the gut-wrenching pain. I could see the blood, and I was slipping away. I turned around to face the perpetrator, but fell to the floor instead, looking up with blurry eyes at two hazy figures, someone in what looked like a pretty pink gown holding a knife dripping with my blood, and a doll-like figure with long brown hair. And with that, I felt my breathing gradually turn shallow as I slowly stopped feeling and everything turned dark.

23

I AM JOSEPH PART I

by Manish Nair

Prologue

Joseph Alex was an intelligent, jolly man, blessed with looks that could charm any woman. How rare was that combination? He worked as a criminal lawyer for the past decade and married the love of his life at a pretty early age. But he never thought of it as a mistake or something that happened in haste.

His wife, Meghana, was his entire world. She was an extraordinarily beautiful lady who worked as a teacher in a Business school. Her beautiful brown skin, big eyes, and gentle personality made her all the more alluring. Everybody adored her. A few agencies had even offered her a modelling photo-shoot when she was in college.

The happy couple lived in a beautiful mansion with their school-going daughter, Neena. She was like no other ordinary child. Just like her parents, she had a special kind of personality that made her everybody's favourite. She was in Grade 6, but she had never met her maternal grandparents more than twice.

Meghana's parents lived on the opposite side of the country but Joseph's mother lived close by. She was the only relative Neena got to visit during her summer vacations. Her parents' families had never gelled that well because of their religious backgrounds, and hence, never had the chance to celebrate the big festivals together. Despite it all, they were a happy, loving family.

But nothing lasted forever, did it? Things were going to change in the next few days for not just Joseph alone, but his entire family. One incident, one decision, and one secret could change a person's life forever.

***

The Beginning

Joseph was on his way to work along with his daughter. He'd drop Neena at school every day. "I love you, my princess, be good." He'd say and kiss her forehead. It had been a ritual since playschool, but now that she had grown into a teenager, she was a little insecure about her friends making fun of her. So now, her father had to kiss her bye before she reached the gate.

The school was just a few blocks away when a bus sped down. In a few moments, a huge noise disrupted the serene morning. The bus had collided with their car. Luckily, the public bus driver had just dropped off all his passengers and was returning to the depot. He wasn't affected much but his bus was in bad shape. But Joseph's driver Rajesh incurred a few fractures and lots of internal bleeding.

Neena was safe without any major injuries, except for a scar above her eyebrow. Unfortunately for Joseph, the accident permanently damaged his eyesight. It was tough to recover from this massive accident, but Joseph, despite his grief, managed to convince Neena that some things were not in their hands.

This was just the beginning of a series of unfortunate events in Joseph's life. A case was filed against the bus driver and a fellow family friend helped them find out the person's details to demand compensation for the loss he had incurred. Even though Joseph was doing pretty well at his job, he had to think twice before spending luxuriously. Money could be a luxury for people like him for a day and become a need for survival the next. Such was the job of a criminal lawyer. But Joseph did not complain even once. He loved his job and the risks it brought. After the court gave its verdict, it was confirmed that there was nothing Joseph could do about the accident.

Turns out, the brakes of the bus had failed, and the driver was unable to bring it to a halt.

***

It was a beautiful Saturday morning. The father-daughter duo was engaged in conversation on the balcony.

"Neena, you shouldn't worry about the past," Joseph said, gesturing Neena to sit beside him. She smiled and looked at her mother sitting by her desk, evaluating assignments.

"I told you, Joseph, something was not right that morning," Meghana said.

"I hate how your instincts are never wrong," he replied.

"You two should visit Mom for a while. Maybe Neena will feel better and you'll get a break, too." Walking towards Joseph, Meghana stroked his hair. "I hate how life treated you despite all that you've done for the world," she said and kissed him on the head.

"I'll call Mom and ask if we can stay for a week," Joseph picked up his phone and dialled in. In a few minutes, the doorbell rang.

"Oh, hey!" Meghana said, opening the door. "You guys reached early!"

"Yeah, there is a new expressway that is about an hour faster," Akshay said, putting down his backpack.

"Wow, Meghana, the interior looks beautiful," Sandeep said and followed Akshay in.

Sandeep and Akshay were Meghana's cousins who had recently moved into the state. They lived in the next city which was about half a day's journey away. They were pretty close ever since childhood, and Joseph used to take Neena to their place for a few days now and then.

Both of them were not married yet. They shared a flat with a third roommate named Leon. They never saw Leon much, since he was away in his hometown every time Joseph's family visited them. Sandeep and Akshay had come to help Joseph and take care of Neena while Meghana would be away at work. "How are you, Joe?" Akshay put his arm around Joseph's shoulder.

"Well, I don't mean to be insensitive, but when you're blind since birth, you don't know the beauty of the earth at all and get used to the darkness, creating a whole new imaginary world in your mind. But how should a man, who has already seen so much of colour, get used to staring into pitch darkness now?" Joseph said. "I understand. It must be so hard for you." Akshay nodded sympathetically as he poured a cup of tea.

"Well, Meghana and I decided that I should visit Mom for a few days. I just got off the phone with her. We'll leave early morning tomorrow. It's a good thing you guys came. I won't have to worry about Meghana being alone."

"That seems like a good idea. Neena will feel better too. We'll be here, no worries." Sandeep said.

They finished their tea and all headed to their bedrooms. Neena helped Joseph walk in and they packed a small bag. She had been a little low the entire week but the excitement of meeting her grandma lifted her spirits. It was pretty late when they finished. Joseph kissed Neena goodnight and she went to her room. Just then, Meghana walked in.

"So, any plans for tomorrow?" He asked, taking off his black glasses.

"No, I think both of them are tired, and I have to work as well, so we'll just stay home. But maybe during the weekend, we'll go to the clubhouse for a game of tennis." She lies down next to him and puts her hands in his hair. "Why did this have to happen to you, my darling?"

"Fate, honey. Sleep now. It's going to be a long day tomorrow," Joseph sighed.

It indeed would be a long day.

***

Darkness

The day seemed to be a beautiful one. Birds chirped a little more happily, the breeze was warm, and the sun was bright, although for Joseph, it was nothing but another day in the dark. Both of them were all set to leave. Their driver, Rajesh, was still hospitalised, so Joseph's neighbour, Dilip, who was also his close college friend, agreed to drive them there and pick them up again next week.

Dilip was a doctor and worked in the same hospital that Joseph was checked into after the accident. He was also of financial help for the family every time they were in need. He even sponsored Neena's literature trip to Jaipur last year, since he was always fascinated by her love for books and reading.

"*Bhabhiji*, are they ready yet?" He called out from the living room.

"They'll be out in a minute. And by the way, thank you so much for this, Dilip," Meghana said, bringing out the bags. Neena's bag was only filled with books and art supplies. "This girl is never going to learn how to travel light!"

"*Jaane do, bhabhi* (Let it go)," Dilip laughed, "At least she'll keep her creativity alive that way."

"But it's just for a week! I wonder if Shakespeare and Ruskin Bond ever took a week off either."

"Neena! Neena!" Joseph called. "I almost forgot my pills. Have you packed them?"

"Yes, Papa. Don't worry. Dilip Uncle, I'm ready, let's go!" Neena said, jumping excitedly.

"The traffic will be bearable only if we move quickly now." Dilip and Neena helped Joseph walk out and get in the car. Meghana, Akshay, and Sandeep stood by the door to wave them goodbye. No one knew that one of them would be saying their last one.

It was a pretty good week for all of them. Meghana was working from home and her cousins spent their time watching IPL and discussing the plan for their new start-up. As for Neena and Joseph, they were enjoying their holiday and were being pampered well with food, sweets, games, and grandma stories. Little did they know what was actually in store for them.

Joseph had an appointment around mid-afternoon the next day. Neena tagged along with him, and both of them took a rickshaw to the hospital. Rajesh was still hospitalised there, so Joseph picked up some fruits and coconut water for him on the way. They almost spent the entire afternoon running one test after the other which Joseph had been asked to and spoke to Rajesh for an hour or two. He was getting better, but the doctor wasn't very happy with his progress. His internal organs were still heavily damaged. By the time they reached home, it was already dark and almost dinner time.

"*Dadi*! We met Uncle Rajesh today," Neena said, jumping into her grandma's lap. "And Papa even bought me a double scoop ice-cream."

Her grandma laughed. "You find a way to have fun even at a hospital, don't you, Neena?" she replied, kissing her.

"She is always excited, Maa," Joseph said, folding his walking stick.

Neena went on to narrate every detail of the day while Joseph made his way to the bedroom. He changed into his pyjamas and settled at the table for dinner. Neena and her grandmother joined him in a few minutes, and the three feasted on the delicious food cooked by Neena's grandma. Neena loved what her grandma made every time and never complained, even if it were sometimes a little too spicy or salty. She loved her a lot and never wanted to hurt her in any way.

They talked and reminisced and before they knew it, time had flown by. Neena hugged her grandma good night and went to bed. Just as Joseph was about to fall asleep, his phone. His hands fumbled at the bedside table, trying to feel and search for the phone. Finally finding it, he felt around and hit the answer button. Thank god for old cell phones.

A deep, hoarse voice on the other line greeted him, "Hello. Is this Mr. Joseph?"

"Yes, this is he," he replied.

"Sir, we found a man here on the road, and we found your number among one of his emergency contacts. It looks like he has been stabbed and I think he is no more…"

24

I AM JOSEPH PART II

by Manish Nair

"Hello. Is this Mr. Joseph?"

"Yes, this is him," Joseph replied.

"Sir, we found a man here on the road – and we found your number among his emergency contacts. It looks like he has been stabbed and I think he is no more..."

***

The Phone Call

Joseph pressed and held a number on his keypad to speed-dial Meghana. In a few rings, she answered, her voice groggy and hoarse. "What happened darling? Is everything okay?"

"Where are Sandeep and Akash?"

"They're working in the study. They were talking about their business when I took them dinner. Is everything fine? You sound so worried. Is Neena okay?" Meghana said.

"Yes, Neena is fine. I have to go, don't worry. I'll call you soon." He disconnected and clumsily felt around for his coat and stick. Carefully stepping out, he heard the rumble of an auto rickshaw and tried to stop it. All the way there, he was shaking his legs. The driver checked on him a couple of times because Joseph sounded too worried every time, he dialled in all his contacts to check if they were alive.

In 20 minutes, he reached the spot. The smell of fresh blood and sweat hung in the air as Joseph found his way to the police radio chatter. He overheard an officer declare having found a wallet. The cards and license belonged to a male, Akash.

"Oh my god... Akash," Joseph gasped. "How did this happen?"

"Who are you?" asked one of the two officers.

"I am Joseph, Sir. I got a call from someone here." Joseph replied.

"Mr. Katti," the man said, and thrust his hand in Joseph's, which the latter felt and grasped. "What is his full name?"

"Akash Kumar."

"How are you related to him?"

"He is my wife's cousin, Sir. He had just come to town."

"Where does he live?" Mr. Katti took out a small notebook and clicked the back of his pen.

"Pune – he moved there for work a few years ago from here." Just as he was asking a few more questions, his partner called out from somewhere far away, "Sir! There is another man here. He's also been stabbed." Joseph's senses rose to alert.

"Oh, man. Looks like I won't be going home soon tonight. I better call my wife, else there will be third corpse tonight," he scoffed. Joseph hung on to every word shared between the police, careful not to miss out. Both the corpses were at a short distance from each other, but the other body looked like it was hidden behind a tree on purpose. There was nothing except clothes on him.

Joseph heard the sound of tires churning against the gravel, and on cue, another car arrived at the scene. He heard Mr. Katti address them respectfully. One of them seemed to be a woman. She asked Mr. Katti about the situation. A minute later, Mr. Katti guided Joseph closer to the body to see if he could identify it. As soon as Joseph touched the second body, he knew who it was.

***

Two Dead Men

"Sandeep Kumar," the policeman wrote down.

"Sir, how can this happen? They were very kind people. I don't remember anyone hating them," Joseph said.

"There are other motives than just hate, Mr. Joseph," he said, squatting by the corpse.

He took out a white handkerchief and pulled out the knife. "Like love, or in this case, burglary." He put it in a zip lock bag and handed it to the other policeman. "Send this to the forensics." He turned towards Joseph again, "What happened to your eyesight?"

"I lost it in an unfortunate accident a few weeks ago."

"That's unfortunate."

"Are you suggesting they were robbed?"

"Looks like it. No wallet or shoes."

Suddenly the woman officer's voice startled him, "No. This isn't as simple as it seems."

"Everything is always as simple as it is, Reena," Katti replied impulsively.

"You haven't changed much."

"Why do people need to change when they like the way they are?"

Joseph stood there, not sure what to say. A few more shreds of evidence from both the bodies were retrieved and sent in zip lock bags. After an hour, Meghana reached the area. Joseph had requested Mr. Katti to call her as soon as the bodies' identities were confirmed. "Oh my god…" She put her palm over her mouth in shock. "What happened here, Joe?"

"Mr. Katti, this is my wife Meghana. Meghana, this is the officer-in-charge for Akash and Sandeep's murder. He has been very kind to me."

Tears pooled in her eyes and Meghana kept brushing them back. "Hello. I wish we could have met under better circumstances. Thank you so much for taking care of my husband."

"You're not the first to feel that way, ma'am. Most of what I do isn't very pleasant, anyway."

"What time did you talk to them last?" Another policeman drew his book and pen out again.

"At around 9:30 p.m. for dinner. I had ordered takeout food because I had to work late."

"Did one of them receive the parcel?"

"No, I did. In fact, they didn't even come to the table. They were pretty involved in some discussion about their business."

Meghana continued to answer more questions about the exact timings of their whereabouts since they were in town, and if any of them had a spare key to the house.

Not much came out of it, though, so the police requested to search the house. The junior officers were asked to take care of the body and supervise the post-mortem reports. Officer Katti and Officer Reena accompanied Joseph and Meghana back home.

The drive to their house was silent. Meghana made a few calls to her family and some of Akshay's friends. Sandeep barely had any family left. Both his parents had passed away and he was an only child. In a few hours, the big police jeep halted in front of their gate.

"What is this?" Mr. Katti asked, turning towards Meghana. The cops had almost searched the entire house in barely 20 minutes and had turned everything upside down.

The entire cupboard was thrown on the bed and project papers and files Akshay and Sandeep were working on were scattered all over the floor. Meghana was extremely frustrated at the mess but she kept calm. They were in Sandeep and Akash's bedroom with Mr. Katti holding up a piece of garment in Meghana's face.

"That is a bra, Sir," Meghana replied a little uncomfortably.

"Yes, I can see that, ma'am, but whose is it?"

"Uh, I don't know."

"Send this to the forensics and get the DNA traces. See if it matches anyone – especially her."

"They were your cousins, right? What is your bra doing in their room under their beds?"

"I already said that this isn't mine and I have no idea what you're talking about." Silence filled the room by Meghana's tone.

"You cannot talk to my wife like that, Sir," warned Joseph.

"And you cannot talk to anybody like that if you are a suspect, understand?" Mr. Katti snapped back in annoyance.

Tension filled the air as the cops continued their search in the men's room. They picked up most of the things – leftover food, their business files, underwear, and even the toothpicks. A little while later, there was a knock on the main door. Meghana opened it to find Dilip, whom she invited in the living room and explained what had happened. Joseph walked out of the room, tapping his walking stick on the floor.

"I had just spoken to them before going to bed. I can't believe everything happened so quickly," Meghana was saying.

"I wish I was here for you, Meghana," Joseph said and put his arms around her shoulder.

"Clearly they don't think it's a case of robbery, do they?"

"Well, they do, but they need enough evidence to cover that, too."

The three didn't speak much. Once the policemen were done, they sealed the room with yellow tape and asked all family members to remain in town until everything was settled. Mr. Katti left his card with Dilip to make a call or leave a message anytime if needed.

Just when they thought the day couldn't be any worse, their phone rang again.

"Hello. Is this Mr. Joseph?"

Joseph could feel his perspiration trickle down his neck. He knew this wasn't the best hello.

"I'm sorry to tell you this but the man you brought in here a few weeks ago just passed away."

Epilogue

It was 4:30 am and the sun would come up in a couple of hours. Three people had died in the last 6 hours. The forensics had come in. The post-mortem confirmed the time of death to be around late evening and mentioned slight marks of struggle over their body. Meghana had confessed about her affair with Akash and Sandeep. Joseph was devastated but he knew this was coming. All those nudes he saw on her phone wasn't just for him. The cops found Meghana's DNA on both the corpses and a bag of 20 lakhs on the scene of crime. The chats on her phone were with Akash to hand in all the money to her because she said she was a better choice for her startup. She had asked for 51% of the shares and Akash denied giving her even half of it. All the evidence pointed against her now. The case was taken forward to court and it was believed that Meghana killed both her cousins for the money and position. She was given a life term sentence to prison. The driver, Rajesh, had struggled for 4 hours in coma before he passed away. The city remained quiet to Neena and Joseph ever since. They got along and moved on from all the pain and silence in the family.

***

5 Years Later

Neena was in high school now. Meghana was in jail and Joseph had been divorced for more than three years now. Mr. Katti received a tape that day. He looked at the parcel and a sticky note on it.

I'm sending this to you, hoping you will understand.

Thank you, Mr. Katti, for everything.

— Joseph Alex

The tape played.

"Hi. I am Joseph. I am the father of Neena Joseph. I was never a man of violence. But I am the cause for the death of three people. And I am not guilty.

Akshay and Sandeep had been sleeping with my wife ever since we were married. They were all three lying bastards. I'd come home from work and she'd be all covered in cologne and she'd tell me she wore it because she missed me. Crazy, because I never wore cologne. About our driver Rajesh – one day Neena came up to me and started crying. When

I confronted her she told me that Rajesh had tried to get up her skirt the day he was dropping her off to school alone and threatened her to not tell anyone. He did that more than once. That disgusting pig tried to touch my princess. My princess! He'd definitely have to die. I staged that accident and pretended to be blind. My daughter still has no idea that I have seen her grow into such a beautiful girl. I will be operated in a few days, and then, they'll think I have my eyes back. Thanks to Dilip for understanding and helping me get through this. Meghana, my love, I always loved you. No matter what you did to me, I will always love you. That is why I have spared your life.

Yes, I am owning up to my sins.

I am Joseph. And I did this for my daughter."

25

THE EXTERMINATION OF RASHID KUNJU

by Manoj Vaz

The following story is an excerpt from the novel TINSEL by the same author. It is available in paperback and Kindle editions on Amazon.in

***

Her name was Shabnam Ansari and she had just turned sixteen. But she went by the name of Tulsi and was one of the most popular bar dancers at Ricardo Bar in Chembur, a central suburb of Mumbai.

Hailing from a village called Barwa in the outskirts of Dhaka, Bangladesh, her parents along with her three younger siblings had illegally migrated to Calcutta. But with no way to make ends meet, Tulsi had come to Bombay with a tout and found work at Ricardo Bar as a dancer.

Tulsi was a tall, slender, good-looking girl and incredibly mature for her age. Dancing at Ricardo Bar was a stop-gap arrangement for her. She knew she was better than that and had always harboured a secret desire to be a film actress. She also had the maturity to realize that she still had a lot to learn and must wait for the opportune moment.

Life was good at Ricardo. All she had to do was make eye contact with the inebriated customers, mostly married men with fat wives and unhappy marriages, swaying to chart-bursting Bollywood tunes while pointing at them as they would immediately loosen their purse strings and shower her with love; here, love being 10 Rupee notes.

On average, she earned thirty thousand rupees a month after giving the middle-aged Sadanand Shetty, the owner of Ricardo, his cut. The amount was enough to provide for the rent of her quarters in a chawl located nearby Govandi area, which she shared with 3 other girls. She could also manage to money-order ten thousand rupees to her family in Calcutta every month.

"Men are stupid," her colleague Rashida had astutely advised her, "keep them hanging and they will lavish their riches on you. But if you give in, they'll treat you like a whore." Tulsi was smart enough to be a sponge to the wisdom of her more experienced colleagues. Most customers were easy to handle. But her objection was Rashid Kunju, a dreaded gangster from Govandi, another central suburb of Mumbai.

Kunju had recently switched allegiance to a Dubai-based don's gang who had entrusted him with the task of extorting businessmen, mostly real estate developers, from the area. Quite besotted with Tulsi, Kunju was at Ricardo every evening at 8:00 pm, like clockwork. He would then shower his newly earned riches on her as she swayed and sashayed for him, all the while cajoling her to spend the night with him.

Tulsi was repulsed by the ugly brute of a man but played along, promising a lot but delivering nothing. Recently, after his newfound gang alliance and subsequent power, Kunju had become more aggressive and quite unbearable to Tulsi. Moreover, she was losing customers because an inebriated

Kunju would pick up fights with any other customer who patronised her. Even the bar owner had threatened to kick her out because of the nuisance created by Kunju.

So, when two young film producers met her with a proposition, she was quite receptive. Kunju was trying to extort them and instead of paying him, they had made a deal with the Mumbai Police Anti-Extortion Cell instead to get rid of his menace permanently. They had realized that it would be a one-time cost, whereas Kunju would be a perennial irritant.

Assistant Commissioner of Police, Kaviraj Chavan, was 40 years old and a 1985 Indian Police Service (IPS) cadre. He had just been transferred from Beed, a district in interior Maharashtra, to helm the AEC in Bombay. Kaviraj was extremely ambitious and had a reputation for being a tough taskmaster. The fact that he was related to an ex-Chief Minister along with his daredevilry in gunning down dacoits in the outskirts of Beed made him one of the youngest ACPs in the state.

Kaviraj courteously heard them out. A deal was struck, and a two-bedroom apartment in the premium Golf Course area of Chembur was in the process of being transferred in the name of Mrs. Suneela Chavan, Kavi's mother.

Now, they needed someone to lure Kunju into the AEC trap. That was where Tulsi came into the picture. The producers had Kunju under the surveillance of a private eye and caught on to his captivation with her. A little homework on Tulsi also gave them an idea of her ambitions. In exchange for setting Kunju up, they promised to get Tulsi enrolled in Mumbai's top acting institute and then a role in their next production.

Tulsi's mind was racing. She had the perfect opportunity to kill two birds with one stone. She could get rid of a major irritant in her life and start the career she had always dreamt of. Yet, she knew she had the opportunity for more. "I will set Kunju up for you, but I need you to do something else too before I do it," she said, "I want you to make a Ration Card for me in the name of Tulsi Mukherjee with a Mumbai address."

The producers immediately contacted a tout, got him to grease the right palms, and procured Tulsi a Ration Card in three days. She was now a resident of Mumbai and a citizen of India. All it cost was Rs. 10,000 and the right contacts. On receiving her Ration Card, an overjoyed Tulsi asked, "Okay, what do you want me to do?"

It was the twelfth of September 2001. Rashid Kunju was in a good mood. All day, the news channels were showing videos of the two airliners smashing into the World Trade Centre twin towers in New York and reducing the iconic power centre of capitalism to rubble. Kunju had nothing to do with Al Qaida or its leader Osama Bin Laden. But the fact that a Muslim terror group had brought the mighty USA to its knees made him smile. "Allah is great," he thought as he smiled, "now the capitalist infidels in Mumbai will also be terrified to receive a call from a Muslim gangster!"

During the day, he made calls to half a dozen targets as they watched the news in horror. He even succeeded in making a few deals. That evening, he strode into Ricardo with an exaggerated swagger. As usual, he had a couple of his henchmen with him. Half a bottle of whiskey and a more than usually flirtatious Tulsi swelled his pride and shrunk his common sense.

At around midnight, when he was holding her hand and trying to pull her to him and paw her, she coyly whispered in his ear, "Not here. Hotel Highway, Room 302. The room is already booked. Wait for me there, I will finish up and reach in an hour." Kunju couldn't believe his luck. After a couple more celebratory drinks, he strutted out with his cronies to his Maruti Omni which he had newly acquired from one of his hapless targets. He even tipped the guard who saluted him elegantly and opened the car door for him, a handsome Rs. 50.

Hotel Highway at Thane, just outside Bombay city limits, was a thirty-minute drive from Chembur at that hour. With music blaring, they reached the dimly lit, deserted Hotel. It was 2:00 a.m. The front office executive, a young shady-looking man, smiled at Kunju and handed over the keys to Room 302 to him. No registration was required when you rented rooms by the hour. "Send half a dozen beers and some light snacks to the room," Kunju snarled. The somewhat long drive and the polluted Bombay highway air had sobered him up.

"Sure Sir," the executive replied, and barked the order to an even shadier looking man lurking in the corner. Still humming a popular Bollywood tune, Kunju got into the lift along with his accomplices.

Once they entered the room, Kunju instructed the others, "We have half an hour before that bitch arrives, let's polish of the beers by then," he then continued in the same breath, "once she arrives, both of you go down and wait for me in the car."

"Yes, Bhai," said one, and the other nodded with a smile.

"Today is the best day of my life," Kunju laughed, "now let me relieve myself and make some space for the beer," and headed to the washroom. Still humming, Kunju peed. Alcohol had messed up his aim and he made an unholy pool in the washroom. Not that he cared. That was when he heard the doorbell ring. Ah, that must be the beer, he thought happily.

When he came out, still humming, he found both his cronies on the floor with their hands cuffed behind their backs with half a dozen cops aiming their guns at them. Seated on the sofa, smiling and pointing his revolver at him was ACP Kaviraj Chavan.

"This is what happens, when you think with your other head, Kunju," Kaviraj laughed.

"That bitch! I will skin her alive," Kunju growled.

"Yes, yes. Of course you will," the ACP jeered.

They were soon bundled into a police van while one of the constables followed in the trio's Maruti Omni.

"You don't know who you are dealing with. I am not the old Rashid Kunju anymore!" Kunju roared.

"Yes, of course. You are now directly reporting to Dubai." Kaviraj laughed.

"You know, I will be let off first thing in the morning and you will be transferred to some Naxalite area!" Kunju thundered. Kaviraj was still smiling, unaffected, much to Kunju's chagrin.

Suddenly, the van steered left towards the forest lands of Yeoor Hills in Thane.

"Why are we going towards the forest?" Kunju stuttered, his confidence a bit shaken.

"Oh," replied Kaviraj matter-of-factly, "we got a report of some wild animals lurking near Mr. A. K. Verma's farmhouse in the jungle. You know Mr. Verma right? I believe you had called his son a couple of weeks ago, demanding Rs. 1 crore as protection money."

"He is a dead man!" Kunju swore, "I will kill him and his family with my bare hands."

"You still don't get it, do you?" Kaviraj smiled at him. The icy look in his eyes froze the blood in Kunju's veins.

The next day, the newspapers reported that dreaded gangster and extortionist Rashid Kunju and two of his henchmen Anwar Khan and Abdul "Kutta" were killed in an encounter with the Police at Yeoor Hills of Thane. The Anti-Extortion Cell had received a tip that the gangsters had made an appointment to collect Rs. 1 crore from a prominent builder from his bungalow in the hills.

When challenged, the gangsters had fired four rounds, injuring a constable. The police party had retaliated and shot all three gangsters dead. The operation was led by the newly appointed Anti-Extortion Cell ACP, Kaviraj Chavan.

A couple of decades passed. An established and successful actress now, Tulsi often had nightmares of a snarling Kunju breaking open her apartment door with a sledgehammer and coming after her, but even she realized that it was collateral damage. Kunju had been a God-sent gift for her.

"Just because you live in the gutter, it doesn't mean you can't look at the stars…" she consoled herself.

26

THE 8ᵀᴴ VOW

by Geetika K. Bakshi

isha still remembered the day she came across Shubham Chaturvedi unexpectedly, years after school ended. She couldn't believe this was finally happening. An IIM graduate at twenty-one, just like every young person, Aisha dreamt of her own start-up business.

She had been on her way to someplace important when he had stopped his car in her way, just because minutes back she was about to collide with his car as a result of her rash driving. That had given a start to their story, a story which Aisha wanted to relive for the rest of her life.

Aisha had been furious with him and had wanted to give him a piece of her mind when he had gotten out of the car and angrily marched up to her. "Are you crazy? Do you think this road is your private property?" Aisha forgot what she was going to say as she drank in the sight of him.

His voice had a texture that did things to her. He was extremely handsome and by way of his manner, smart, too. Aisha had stopped paying attention to his scolding as she concentrated on his eyebrows, his lips, the creases on his forehead. His eyebrows looked like they were freshly plucked. He must have been somewhere around 24-25 years old. Aisha couldn't believe her luck. Just then, a frequent click of fingers brought her back. She stood there, flushed in embarrassment. All she could do was apologise and drop her card on his windshield, which had her new start-up details and phone number.

Aisha was neither an atheist nor a theist. She had always believed in a higher power, but up until then, the higher power had been merely a voice at the back of her head. But now, out of nowhere, it had a face – Shubham's. She reached the 'United' coffee house where she had a meeting. Unfortunately, it went in vain as the investor didn't seem to be impressed that much. Just then, she got a call. Sulking, she hit answer.

"Hello, am I talking to Aisha?"

"Yes, this is Aisha."

"Are you into marketing management?"

"Yes sir, may I know who this is?" Aisha asked.

"My name is Shubham. I'm the guy who shouted at you this morning." He paused before adding, "Don't get any ideas, I didn't call you to say sorry."

"Oh please, it's alright," Aisha rolled her eyes, but couldn't help but smile. What a smart mouth. "How may I help you?" She tried to sound nonchalant at best.

"I need to fix up a meeting with you as soon as possible. I need someone who can market my dream business – I mean my wife's dream business. 'Paridhan textiles' meant everything to her. She's no more, and I want to fulfil her dream for her."

Aisha paused for a long time. "Hello? Hello, are you listening?" His voice pierced through her ears.

"Yes, Mr. Shubham," she said, "I can come. Kindly draft a mail about your project and the details. Then drop a text of the address, day, and time. I'll get back to you."

"Sure. Miss Aisha, I hope you understand how much my late wife's dream is important to me."

She got a mail the same evening, followed by a text message with the details of their meeting. He had planned for them to meet on Friday at 2 p.m. at Café Tesu. Aisha grinned. He had chosen her favourite café without even knowing her at all. Hope surged through her veins and she ended up watching two movies in a row.

Friday rolled in, and she was very relaxed and confident to meet the love of her life. This time work was not the priority. From this meeting onwards, her days and nights would be nothing different than the waxing and waning of the moon. She made her efforts to look the best at all times.

A year passed, then another. Shubham was now the owner of "Paridhan Textiles" – India's fastest growing textile brand. It was the celebration of their joint venture. Aisha blushed as she emphasised on 'their'. She took out her best red dress from the wardrobe for the award ceremony. She wanted to look her best tonight. She knew how special the night was going to be.

They both had a lot of fun and were thoroughly appreciated. They were the youngest achievers at the event and naturally stole the spotlight. Aisha couldn't be happier. She had formed a place in Shubham's life, and now, his heart. Finally, her hard work had paid off.

"I've to go to the loo," she told him.

"Sure, darling. I'll wait in the car." He gazed at her longingly, wondering how he had turned out to be so lucky.

10 minutes later, Aisha came out to the sight of Shubham on one knee, with a ring in his hand. "Aisha, will you marry me?"

***

Aisha was on cloud nine tonight. Why wouldn't she be? She had been waiting for this day all her life.

She said yes to the man of her dreams and even Shubham's parents were happy to have Aisha as their daughter-in-law. They always wanted Shubham to move on in his life when he lost Maira.

Today, they both are about to start the journey of their lives together. It's D-Day. They both tie the knot and take 7 auspicious vows – except Aisha takes 8. As she gazes at her groom, she reminisces her journey. She thinks back proudly on how cleverly she had laid down a trap – a trap she had set to have Shubham in her life. Aisha had been 'Loser Aisha' in junior school who used to look at Shubham from behind the pillars. She even remembered being heartbroken at the news of Shubham and Maira dating, and worse when she got to know about their engagement. Maira had to go.

She first worked on herself, then spent days plotting a fine plan. It had been the night of Shubham and Maira's first wedding anniversary when she had been found dead in the bathtub full of roses, which she had decorated for her husband all by herself.

Aisha is brought back to reality as Shubham adorns Aisha's head with red vermilion. They both are each other's from now on and will share all their darkest secrets, except Aisha's secret 8th vow. With each step forward, the scenes play like a movie at the back of Aisha's mind and she smiles to herself. The bell of room service, the bubble bath, the sweet fragrance of lavender, and the complimentary juice she gave to her which had castor oil seeds in it, which did the job – Loser Aisha had finally won.

27

THE MYSTERY OF THE COIN

by Aaron Dsouza

Deadly and truly the femme fatale of the world, Ophiophagus Hannah is a silent and deadly striker," spoke the ophiologist, as he looked into the crowd and spotted a beauty twirling her blonde locks and intently watching him. He had his target.

The killer had moved.

"How about apples on me?" said the beauty, as she lay naked in bed, her lithe figure oozing a sex appeal like no other. The ophiologist got out and cast a loving look to his pet Russell's viper as he started to dice apples, unaware of the deadly snake that had coiled behind him.

Just as the ophiologist turned around with apple slices in his hand, the beauty launched herself at him and pinned him to the countertop, grabbed the snake by the base of its head, and moved in for the kill. After a brief struggle, the ophiologist dropped dead. The beauty dusted herself, cleared the crime scene, and walked away, but not before placing a meticulously clean gold coin in the bedroom at a particular angle.

The killer had struck.

*****

"Sir, we've got a case of an exotic animal on our hand," said the sub-inspector as they peered over the bluish dead body of the ophiologist.

"No, it's cold-blooded murder," the inspector replied as he ate one of the apple slices. Looking at the confused faces of his team, he added, "It's clear as a day. How come an ophiologist, who handles snakes daily, gets bitten by an agitated snake whose fangs are broken? Plus, not to forget the scent of Arqus Ladies. And the killer is," the inspector moved to the kitchen and angled his body to reveal the illusion.

"Erinys," chorused the team in horror as they spotted the ornately designed coin.

*****

"Aleck will catch you, he is a hunter," spoke a voice.

"No, she is smart. She'll get away," spoke another.

"You should continue killing, I say," spoke another.

"You should stop killing," spoke another.

"Just shut up!" yelled the beauty, as she held her head in her hands.

"What's wrong?" asked her brother.

"It's these voices again. It sucks to be so smart," groaned the beauty as her brother comforted her.

"That's funny, you wear the same perfume as my suspect," said the brother.

"Suspect?" she asked as she contently dug into her pilaf.

"Yeah, she won't be able to hide for long," he said with confidence. His sister nodded.

"Shall I drop you at college?" asked her brother as she picked up her bag.

It was an uneventful ride to the college, marred with typical Indian traffic. "Give me a call. I'll come to pick you up if I'm free," the brother said and rode off into the typical Indian heat.

"Hello Catrina, care to join me?" Roshan, a rich tycoon's son, caught up to her.

"No," retorted Catrina as she tried to distance herself, but was held back by Roshan.

"Oh, my darling, you're weak –" Before Roshan could complete his sentence, a loud crack was heard and Roshan fell down, clasping his head in pain.

"What did I tell you? Any rivalry you have, it should be between you and me, not my sister," snarled Aryan, and gently accompanied Catrina to her class. Catrina wore a grateful look as she cast a spiteful, yet intense gaze at Roshan. Aryan wore a knowing and concerned look. He knew.

Someone was marked to hold the skull.

"What good does merely staring down at someone do when you don't even do anything? He's rich and you're too reserved. You don't even hit a mosquito when it sucks your blood," said Arianne, her classmate.

"May I have your perfume?" asked Catrina.

Mors aequo pulsat. (Death knocks).

***

"Chug! Chug! Chug!" encouraged the crowd as Roshan downed an entire bottle of Jack Daniels and smashed the empty bottle on the floor. "Let's party!" he shouted as the DJ dropped the beat and started the music, covering the footsteps of the predator. The hunt was afoot.

The beauty wore a high-slit red dress with a carnival mask as she singled out Roshan from the crowd.

Men were so weak.

The beauty walked up to Roshan with quick steps, and gently, but firmly, pushed in. Roshan gave way to the elusive natural brunette beauty who was taking him for a ride, turning and leading her to his room, where no one would ever know of this midnight ecstasy.

"May I know the name of this beauty?" slurred Roshan as he pinned the beauty to the wall and began to kiss her neck.

"*Requiescat un pace* (Rest in peace)," she whispered as she kissed Roshan and slipped a tablet of pure cocaine covered in duct tape. The stomach would do the rest. The case of cocaine overdose was a common cause of death in such rave parties, estimated to cause death within 5 hours, the onset of dizziness of 20 minutes.

The beauty pushed Roshan as he began to lose control and tried to grasp for support. "Sleep tight, your banal overdrive has caused this," the beauty said, and drained a glass of wine, then left the scene after clearing the crime scene and placing her gold coin, oblivious to the fact that someone was watching, his dog tag gleaming in the moonlight.

Thanatos.

***

"Breaking news, son of rich tycoon dies of an overdose," read Aryan, as everyone shed crocodile tears over Roshan's death for various reasons. Some for his tyranny, some for their parties, or their shopping, while some for their status. Everyone blamed the drugs, but only two people knew the actual reason. Aryan stared at Catrina, then walked over to her and slipped a note, and walked away. Catrina opened the note and stared at it blankly.

Scio (I know).

It was time for the drapes.

Si vis pacem, parabellum. (If you want peace, prepare for war.)

***

"What is this lethargy? Somehow, we got the media to report it as an overdose. Now, explain!" barked the commissioner as he scratched his tattoo and lit his pipe, while Aleck stood, trying to piece together the disparate dots.

"Sir, there is a courier for you," the helper handed Aleck an envelope and left.

"Who sent it?" asked the commissioner as he walked over to the coffee dispenser.

"It's the killer," said Aleck in surprise, as he tore open the seal and looked at the ornately designed coin and the black spot at the top right corner of the card.

"Pirates," said the commissioner cryptically, as Aleck understood the reference.

"What's that tattoo about?" asked Aleck.

"Oh, this is the union of the male and female energies; nine triangles and fifty-four points of intersection. The tattoo artist had to practice so that he didn't screw me over," chuckled the commissioner.

"Now it makes sense," said Aleck, and much to the confusion of the Commissioner, continued, "The killer is not the actual killer, rather a twisted set-up. The intention is someone else's but the act is carried out by another. There is no trace because the killers are different. Evident from the fact that it was a blonde and brunette with the same modus operandi, now I am their target after 8 murders – the last and final one."

"The ninth symphony," said the commissioner cryptically as he snuffed his pipe.

***

"O Freunde, nicht dyes Táne!
Sondern lasst uns angenehmere
anstimmen und freudenvollere.
Freude! Freude!"

The music resonated from the gramophone as Catrina danced, ignoring her brother's look as he rushed in, grabbed his gun, and rushed out, and their eyes briefly met. Catrina twirled around the house. The guns wouldn't matter. This had been a fight of attrition.

Catrina picked up her phone and dialled a number. Three rings and it cut. The signal was sent. Catrina inwardly gleamed at the sight of the act she was going to commit.

*****

Aleck did not notice a 69' Mustang with an inverted torch on its nameplate tail him as he was busy joining the dots. He began to revisit the scenes of murder and their reports.

A 29-year-old male - suicide

A 25-year-old male - overdose

A 20-year-old female - accident

A 19-year-old male - shock

A 24-year-old transgender - satanic sacrifice

A 23-year-old female - mysterious circumstances

A 22-year-old male - snake bite

A 19-year-old male - overdose

All of the victims after the transgender had connections with the Bratva, the organized crime mafia, suggesting a change in motive, but Thanatos was supposed to be dead and the Bratva was under observation. No! It couldn't be a coincidence. Aleck picked up his phone and rang up the Commissioner. "Sir, Erinys and Thanatos are…" Aleck trailed off as he was rammed by a car and thrown off his bike. Aleck immediately recovered and pointed his gun, the sight horrifying him.

Catrina walked alongside a man whose scarred visage reminded Aleck of one man only. Thanatos.

"I understand that you have many questions racing through your mind," Thanatos spoke with a heavy undertone as he sat on the road, while Catrina stood emotionless. Aleck counted his breaths.

"You see, we are a different breed of humans, ones that have evolved for killing and surviving. We chose the Greek line as we are from Greece. Catrina is my lovechild. When that commissioner killed me, he adopted Catrina in hopes to tame her killer instinct, but the result is there," he said and jerked his head to the side. Aleck knew what was coming. The prognosis was negative. Catrina walked over to him and placed a gun and smiled.

"Stop where you are, throw your guns, or your protégé dies," bellowed the commissioner as they dragged Aryan and pointed their guns at him as everything became dead silent.

A gunshot rang out.

28

SCARLET SHIP

by D. H. Holmes

Her lips were the brightest thing in the building. Sure, they were purple, and the building was built in 1882. But still.

I thought it was a harbinger for the kind of weekend in store. 'Her' is Aria. She's Fijian-Indian, the sort with jewels for eyes; who, one might imagine, spends her evenings gazing into a crystal ball.

Ironically, though, we met in a call centre with way too much daylight. An unremarkable beginning, but 18 months later, we're living together in Sydney's inner west. Indeed, the apartment came before the romance, but things have blossomed along nicely and here we are at the 'weekend away' stage. She passed her driving test, pre-corona, and after a little persuasion, was willing to set about the motorway for the first time and ferry us up to the Blue Mountains.

For those who dwell beyond the borders of New South Wales, the Blue Mountains are a sizeable range to the west of Sydney, beyond which lies the sprawling Australian Outback. 90 minutes from the city by car, and generally a hotspot for the folk whose first language isn't English, the name is derived from the blue haze which permeates the bush in every which way, rising from interminable Eucalyptus. It all works - the sprawling backbone of mountain stamped against crystal blue.

Katoomba is the main town, home to the fabled 'Three Sisters'; a natural rock formation which time wrestled into three rather sinister-looking monoliths. Not too far away, stands The Lord Carrington, a.k.a. 'The Grand Old Lady', a 19th-century hotel which I briefly introduced. Her doors opened in 1883, before a courtyard of horse-drawn carriages and fine-looking gentlemen with shoes like mirrors. But nowadays, she stands in the bowels of the modern village, although the charm of yesteryear remains; one only has to cross the threshold of the main entrance to feel like he ought to swap his bags for a top hat and cane.

I confess, hardly have I been privy to such etiquette, but after two or three pale ales at the reception, I dare to return the charming smiles and compliant nods from staff and punters alike, most of whom are dressed head to toe in black, and pretty soon, I'm enamoured by the whole charade; I stride through the grandiose hallways, returning the steadfast gaze of countless portraits up high. I begin to wonder if I ever existed in the modern world, for the sense of belonging is uncanny.

Aria and I soon come upon a sparkling dining hall complete with a Steinway; the muffled melodies of which tease us whilst we peer in through the glass. On the far side, the wall is buried in mountains of trophies; a treasure trove of untold delight. My heart blazes with pride as if they were mine. I pour over the bronze like a child; slack-jawed and wild-eyed with both hands against the glass.

I know that not only do I belong here, but I always have.

Aria has changed into a floor-length dress, and in her dark eyes, I watch the chandeliers twist and sparkle. Taking her arm, I insist, "Come, we must dine here." After a courtly meander, hat-tips, and tight-lips, we secure the last table. By now we're used to the omnipresent scent of mahogany and old cigarette smoke. Our waiter wears a mask; the only clue that 21st-century laws still apply in here and we eat lamb and drink wine until our hearts sing (hardly exchange a word lest we miss a note on the Steinway). A chivalrous affair, entirely! The pianist is impeccable, and Aria swears he could be my double, were he not 50 years my senior, ha! Bloated and merry, we retire to the hallway in search of our room, and once there, dog-tired from the excitement, the pair of us are out before the lantern.

***

Morning brings lemony sunshine and pancakes with fresh cream. Daylight half-brings the place back to the modern era. Alas, I won't say the candour is gone, but without the remarkable pianist and the matador of night, whose silent cape veiled us from the world at large, allowing our imaginations to take hold, the place could be a three-dimensional *Cluedo* board (albeit smokier and with better etiquette).

We check out and hit the road in the roaring Australian sun, and a half-hour later, I might be persuaded that the whole thing was a dream, if not for the evidence on my lap: after checking out, we had wandered into Katoomba and had come upon a self-proclaimed old and rare crystal merchant: Mr. Pickwick's. Inspired by Aria's eye for a good crystal, we had entered a room that wouldn't look out of place in the Carrington, the only difference being the sparkling sapphires and wild turquoises beaming from the display cabinets.

I took care of my footing, for every step threatened to level the display, leaving Aria to her own devices. Instead, I wandered into the books, of which there were few. Then, much to my delight, she was ready to leave. Not wanting to offend the elderly Pickwick, I picked up a red velvet hardback for whose title I had to hunt and purchased it for a reasonable price.

We get home in one piece but later, I lay awake, next to the sleeping Aria, with a melancholy heart. It won't shake. Though I was only at the Carrington half a day, I feel as if my heart and soul were forged from the very thing.

Besides, I'm yet to mention the most significant event, which, after having just woken up (after finally dropping off), I could not swear as to whether took place solely in my imagination: After we left the dining hall, at the Carrington, with our bellies full; I swung jovially around the bannister in preparation for the ascent up the main stairwell. Admittedly, my arc was a little too wide, and definitely spurred somewhat by the bottle and a half with dinner, thus my low swinging head caught the attention of a familiar face in the shadows, seated in a room so dark the face was barely visible. It was the pianist.

Hastily, I aborted my bannister acrobatics and headed over, giving the door a gentle nudge to make space for a proper greeting, and offered my congratulations on a fine evening. Two things startled me: the pianist's voice; whose rich timbre surely belonged to a career tenor, yet his appearance showed a man not far off a hundred. And second, another face in the shadows, an apparent guest opposite him, very much his feminine equal with voice and tea set to match. What followed was a courteous inquiry into my heritage; interestingly, he, too, was British.

Once my purpose was served, which, far as I could tell, was to humour and perplex in equal bouts, I was dismissed but suspected I would remain on their lips far longer than the tea. They were oddly intrigued and wanted a blow-by-blow account of my movements before our meeting.

Back home, as the days roll on, I find myself curiously drawn to the pianist and can seldom stop my mind wandering his way, from which the only real distraction is the red-velvet hardback: Scarlet Ship. Which, it turns out, is captivating in its own right. Were it not the unfolding narrative that compels me to keep my nose in it, the smell of history which leaps upon opening surely does so. Simply put, it reminds me of The Carrington.

I wish the comparison would end there, for the lines between fiction and reality are becoming awfully hazy. There are startling similarities between the book's narrative and that of my own experience in Katoomba last weekend. Indeed, one of the characters is a retired tenor-come-pianist and the novel itself is set in mountains named after their colour! Even the protagonist is my age. I almost forget about Carrington and the pianist, instead get utterly enveloped in the puzzle of this book – the author of which apparently escapes even the internet! R.C Finney: Published in London between the wars. Mostly with Partridge. That's the extent of my knowledge. But the mystery of it all is a splinter in my soul; other than the book's bloody ending, the rest of it could well be written about me.

The following Tuesday, I book the Carrington. There are things I must confirm for the sake of my sanity. I'm convinced I exist in two realities; one in the here and now, writing this sentence, and the other as a retired tenor-come-pianist within the halls of the Carrington. The mysterious Scarlet Ship is some kind of fulcrum between the two worlds.

Aria wants nothing to do with it. She won't tag along, and my obsession has driven her to pack a bag. "Darling, are you listening to what I'm saying? Do you realise the implications?" I'm screaming, shaking the book at her.

"Rupert, please stop. Stop all this, you must!"

"The pianist and I… we're…"

So be it. I alone must resolve this personal crisis.

***

With *Scarlet Ship* underarm, I board at Sydney Central. The Carrington welcomes me like an old friend, and this time, I figure why she bears her alias: *The Grand Old Lady*. She has a charm seldom found in women of my generation, and the resolution of a mature longing settles upon her embrace. I'm in. Here we go again, shiny staffs and curt smiles. Bashful glances from ladies-under-hat; the lickety-clak of heels on wood. Unseen chatter.

In the Grand Ballroom, I set to work and enquire about the pianist. The bartender gives me a maddening shock: 'Who, Mr. Finney?' *What?!* They bear the same name? Wild theories take flight in my imagination. Another remarkable coincidence. There are powers at play beyond my understanding. Thus, my quest to find the pianist, a.k.a. 'Finney', borders on feverish. I comb the building till sundown, quizzing every man and dog, trying every room to which I have access (admittedly not the 'King George' or 'Lord Carrington' rooms). Nothing.

Dishevelled, but by no means dejected, I return to my suite on the third floor. The mystery deepens, but my passion is equal to the task. There's little else I can do at this hour, save taking a fire-axe to the locked doors, so I resolve to waiting till morning. *See you at breakfast, old boy.*

Aria's Nikon bulges from my bag strewn on the bed. Fortune favours me! Under the guise of a building inspector, I stalk the corridors on the off-chance I catch Finney out of bed. The corridors are lit by lanterns whose shadows flicker long behind, and the place has taken on a ghoulish quality, I admit.

Silently, I wander, half-expecting to come upon Finney grinning in the shadows. I close my eyes and search with my ears. A nearby owl tells me it is late. The camera around my neck, I come to the dining hall and cross into the blackness. Memory fills in the shadows with tables and chairs and for the most part, I move unopposed.

My thigh meets a chair, which resounds in the eerie void. It is truly black; I can't make out the trophy cabinet. Lest I send it reeling! An idea strikes me like a match: the camera. I point and shoot at the void, and the room lights up like lightning, clicks echoing like a thunderclap. Alarmed and knocked off balance, I end up scrapping with a tablecloth for the exit. Surely I've gone too far; a tornado would've done less damage on the way out.

Feverish, I somehow make it upstairs, toss the camera on the bed and pace up and down, cursing my nerve.

Where is he?

Wait. I check the camera and the image takes my soul. Beneath a chandelier, in the middle distance, lurks an unmistakable face amidst the tables and chairs; a ghostly spectre with eyes blood-red: Finney! Caught by the bootstraps of adrenaline, I descend the spiral staircase and burst into the great dining hall. *Point and shoot. Point and shoot.*

***

Finney

The flash blinds me but the deed is already done. Pungent kerosene, a glimmering blade. By lantern light, I stare into the terrible face of my pursuer: the young enigma who haunts my dreams; he must be three generations my junior! An ode to his passion, I stay with him till the end: thick claret pulses from the wound in his throat, weaker with every heartbeat.

When it is done, I drag him with the strength of a man of his years and his rigid fingers still clasp the blood-spattered camera.

For what purpose photograph me? Under cobbled archways whose secrets are known to few, we leave a trail of deepest red. To a place where candles are already lit and long limp shadows twist and ebb; the only spectators to a grim finale. Onto a heap whose nethermost recesses are bonier than their fleshier apex.

First, they show up in my dreams, and then, they end up *here*. Always the same, and I know that somewhere upstairs, a red velvet hardback awaits. Must I return it to Pickwick *again?*

Maybe I'll hang onto it this time; the years have usurped much of my memory, but I could swear it is written in *my* hand.

29

GOLDFISH

by Sudha Ramnath

Interrogation is nothing but a fishing expedition. Just like the sport, an inquiry also needs a lot of patience. You cast the bait and wait patiently for the fish to get caught. That's exactly what I had been doing for the last few hours. But this particular fish just wouldn't take the bait.

Let me tell you about Vatsala Devi, the writer who suddenly took the world by the storm. The 65-year-old author was slotted to win a Booker, no less! As she sat in front of me, I could see that with a puckering, pointed mouth, she did resemble a fish. She seemed to have a proclivity for gold. There was gold around her neck, slipped on to her wrists and on her ears and nose. I immediately nicknamed her 'Goldfish'.

Last month, we got a call from the Dehradun police station. Apparently, there was an ancient guest house in the hill station that was being demolished. No one had been living there for years and finally, someone had bought it. While trying to rebuild it, they found a dead body buried in the garden. The body had withered down to a skeleton, indicating that the person had been dead for a long time.

The inspector in-charge checked the missing persons' files and found that a twenty-year-old girl called Mallika, an orphan, had been reported missing. The matron at the orphanage remembered her as a very smart and ambitious girl who dreamed of becoming a writer. The clothes and the plastic jewellery on the skeleton confirmed that the body was Mallika's. The police checked the date of the missing person report with who stayed at the guesthouse at that time and came up with the name of Vatsala Devi or VD as she is known in her circles.

VD stuck to her story. She had gone to Dehradun to write her first novel when she was around 22 years old. Mallika was a local girl, educated and smart. She had offered to type VD's novel daily, as it was the 70's and there were no computers. She had typed the last page and handed over the completed book, placed in a file. On the very next day, VD had left for Delhi. She had never heard anything from Mallika after that.

I baited her, teased her, taunted her, and irritated her. But my goldfish did not budge or rise to the bait. But I was determined not to let this one slide out of my grip.

A couple of days later, VD called me, asking me over to her palatial bungalow. As I waited, I saw a huge aquarium placed prominently in the living room. Her personal secretary was changing the water in the aquarium and was trying to catch the exotic fish with a net and place them in a bowl of water. But one goldfish in the tank was giving him a lot of trouble. Just like VD, I thought. It kept escaping the net and played about. With difficulty, he caught it and put it into a huge bowl along with the others. Next, he changed the water and put all the fish back.

From the window, I could see the gardener digging up the earth and making a hollow pit in the ground. VD joined me soon. It looked like there was more gold on her person than last time. After some small talk, she went in and brought some tea for me. I wasn't a big fan of tea, but she insisted on it because it was her 'special' tea. She waited till all her staff had left before starting on her narrative, "Inspector, I want to tell you a story. After all, I am a writer!" She gave a smile that looked more evil to me than genuine.

"But mind you, it has nothing to do with me or my life. I know you have been digging for more and more information about me. I thought I would explain everything to you before – " She seemed to be keenly watching me. Maybe she wanted some kind of validation for whatever she wanted to say. I kept a neutral expression and continued to listen. "– before you make any decisions."

I couldn't figure out if it was the stuffy atmosphere in the room, but I was feeling a little breathless and disoriented. She began to look more and more like a fish. I mentally shook myself and tried to give her all my attention.

"There was this very smart girl who loved to write and was blessed with a lot of creativity. Let's call her M. Even though she was very ambitious, she never got any exposure to take her writing into the world because she lived in a small town in Dehradun." There was total silence in the room. Only the whirr of the AC could be heard. Despite that, I had started to sweat.

"Once, a rich and upcoming writer, let's call her V, came to town and used M's services to type out what she wrote. M realised that V did not have many talents and what she wrote was mediocre. They slowly became friends when they realised that both of them were orphans." I sat straighter on the sofa. I seemed to have slid down a little. VD continued to tell me her story.

"M had given a lot of suggestions and the book was turning out to be excellent despite V's mediocrity. It was the final day of work and M had finished typing the last chapter. M was supposed to go back home, put all the chapters into a file and bring it back the next morning."

I was feeling very tired and was losing track of what VD was saying. She left her seat and came to sit right next to me on the sofa.

Was it the light or were my eyes playing a trick on me? Her sophisticated-writer look seemed to have deserted her. Her face looked like some gothic, grotesque fish with a grouse.

"M went into the kitchen and made some tea for V. Just like you, V did not want to drink it. But M insisted and made sure V finished the cup of her 'special' tea. The next day, M came with the finished manuscript. She found V lying dead on the sofa, exactly where she had left her. She had been dead for a long time. There was froth around her mouth from the poison M had added to the tea."

As she continued her narration, VD's voice seemed to have gained a new edge. As if she was gloating over the memory as she recounted her story.

"M had realised how easy it would be for her to become V. How easy it would be for her to become an author using V's money and fame. Both of them were of the same age and looked similar. She had gone about planning everything meticulously. Those days, there were no Aadhar cards or ID proofs. She exchanged clothes and accessories with the dead body, buried it in the garden, took a taxi, and left for Delhi. She soon moved to Mumbai and became a celebrated author. After all, she did have a lot of talent."

She took a napkin and delicately wiped something from around my lips. By then, I was losing consciousness.

As I slid onto the floor, I could see the goldfish staring at me. Was it in the tank or was it sitting next to me? As I thrashed on the floor, the last thing I remembered was the pit the gardener had dug in the garden.

30

LOVE FOR THE GAME

by Uma Bokil

Delhi

Samar

I hated the din of the club. The bass was making my head throb, and hordes of people huddled together, dancing, were making me claustrophobic. For the umpteenth time, I felt glad about having gotten a floor for private dining and booths built above this zoo. The club would soon go, too, and then, I wouldn't have to witness these good-for-nothing children wasting their lives in booze and the after-effects of their hangovers. This place could use some class.

Joe caught up to me, his eyes constantly darting in every direction. The rest of his skittle dolls in black uniforms enveloped me from all sides as usual. "Six missed calls from Sehgal. Again," he said.

"Any message saying what he wants?"

Joe smirked. "Sehgal and texting? Really?"

I chuckled and tried to bee line my way to the dining above, but college groupies had blocked the entrances of both the flights of stairs. Just as I struggled to ascend one, I heard catcalls and hooting from the dance arena. I turned my neck to the right, about to pass a comment about the lack of civility but stopped in my tracks. Suddenly, the chaos didn't matter. I could neither hear the bass, nor the deafening noise people these days called music; nor could I breathe. All I could do was stare agape at her.

She was dressed provocatively in red, her dress just the right amount of short that it didn't make her look indecent, yet enough to show off her slender, toned legs. She was swaying to the music alone. I'd never seen a person look so complete in their mere existence. She was moving vivaciously and sensually, occasionally moving her hands through her hair, as if she were under a spell, intoxicated by her own vibrancy, and I were a mere fragment caught up in her resonance.

I moved towards her, suddenly wishing it were my hands moving through her hair, holding her, caressing her. She noticed me making my way over. I was so focused on her face that I could even see her mouth curl up into a smirk from afar. The smirk turned into a breath-taking grin as I closed off the distance, and she sashayed her hips flirtatiously.

With ease, I slipped my arm around her perfect waist, pulling her close to me. Our noses touching, we gazed at each other's lips, hers stunningly bow-shaped and full. Her eyes carried a sweet yet lustrous dominance. The only thing that broke the hex I seemed to be under was the song slowly fading out to an end.

"Liked what you saw?" She smiled seductively, her eyes boring into mine.

"If you'd join me, I'd show you just how much." She looked at me quietly for a minute, worrying me that she'd say no.

"I'd like that," she said at last, and I caught myself sighing in relief.

I guided her back to where my men were waiting, and we climbed upstairs. Finally nestling in a booth far off in a corner, Joe and his squad scattered around the place to engage security.

Making herself at home, she ordered a whiskey, neat, while I asked for a Scotch on the rocks with a twist.

"Well, not that I'd mind calling you 'gorgeous' all night, but I'd love to know your name," I said, casually wrapping my arm around the seat.

"Who said I was going to be here all night?"

I blinked at her, at a loss for words. Why did I say that?

"I'm kidding!" she laughed. "Oh, the look on your face."

My insides swooned at the sound of her laugh.

"I'm Zeya," she said finally. She smiled again, but this time, it had a warmth that made me stare at her all over again.

"And you?" she asked.

"Excuse me?"

"What's your name?"

Two of my men who were within earshot whisked their heads in our direction, their faces contorted with flabbergast. That was a question I hadn't been asked in a couple of years.

"I –"

"You look so cute when you're shocked," she laughed again. "You're Samar Ahuja, CEO and Founder of Ahuja's Designs, the renowned Interior Design Consultancy firm. You bought this club, turned it into a chic restaurant, and are one of the youngest self-made billionaires in the country. Did I get that right?" She winked. "I read a lot." Her eyes sparkled.

I grinned. Who was this woman?

We engaged in an easy flow of conversation over drinks, and I found myself intrigued by her with each passing minute.

"So, Zeya, what do you do?"

"I'm a lawyer," she replied simply. "Although, I do love partying."

I turned to her. "Then I assume you know all the right places."

"Maybe. Why?"

"According to you, what would make a club the hotspot for the elite public? Take the club downstairs for example." She squinted at me in confusion, obviously thrown off by the randomness of my question.

"I've renovated a lot of places, but clubs are my debut," I explained. "I thought I'd dive into the public eye. Sometimes, the best things are too obvious to the eye to be noticed."

"Well, let's see. I'd lose the DJ, get a live band – you know, jazz, Latin, blues. I'd keep the dance floor, make this an exclusive membership-only club, and extend fine dining downstairs for formal dinners and cocktail parties. A place this posh could lose its charm to these horrible songs and this horrible crowd. Oh, and the interior desperately needs a change. This place could use some class."

I sat there, grinning ear-to-ear. "What?" She frowned.

Still grinning, I lifted her in my arms and took her to bed.

***

A week later, I was heading out when my phone rang.

"On my way, Mr. Sehgal. Yes. No, don't do anything unless I get there. Uh-huh. Okay." I quickly hung up. I read the email I received the previous afternoon from one of our top investors for the tenth time.

Herman and Co. had been one of our investors for ages. They had recently planned an employee retreat at my resort in Miami which had gone horribly awry. Apparently, the hospitality and management were abhorrent, and room service was as though it were a motel – both of which I found implausible. And now, they wanted to sue.

I arrived at The Greene Hotel at five minutes to noon for my lunch appointment with Sehgal.

"Reservation under Mr. Sehgal," I told the maître d'.

"Right this way, Mr. Ahuja. Mr. Sehgal is already here."

Sehgal looked years older than I'd seen him last. Cancer was never a good thing. After a handshake and a brief hug, we ordered lunch and cut to the chase.

"Get this. Herman and Co.'s accusations are way over the line," Sehgal began.

"Thought so," I murmured. "So, what exactly did happen?"

"One of the waiters spilled a drink on one of their employees during an important dinner. Sometime later, the same waiter stumbled while serving dessert and spilled hot chocolate sauce on three people. A lady was furious because the hot sauce reddened her skin. Also, our Thai massage facility didn't exactly feel Thai."

I groaned. "Get us out of this, please."

"I will. On one condition."

"Which is?"

He gave me the same sheepish look which I'd come to recognise for quite some time. Realisation dawned upon me.

"Mr. Sehgal, you know I highly respect you and your daughter must be really charming but –"

"Please, just meet her. I invited her over. She's your age, pretty, smart – you know, like me." I couldn't help but smile.

"All the same, I really wish you hadn't –"

"Dad?" said a familiar voice.

Sehgal's gaze moved past me, and he smiled warmly. Turning around in my chair, my jaw dropped as I stared unblinkingly, disbelievingly at Zeya. Grinning, she walked to our table. She was dressed in formals, looking stunning, a complete contrast to the woman I'd met at the club, and yet, so alluring.

"Hi, I'm Zeya." She extended her hand.

I gaped at her, dumb founded. What was she doing?

"Told you she was pretty," Sehgal smiled. "Anyway, you kids catch up. I need to use the restroom."

I kept smiling till Sehgal was out of sight, then turned to her. "You're Zeya Sehgal?"

"Guilty," she smiled sheepishly. "Speaking of, could you not tell him we've already met?"

"Wow, was the night that bad?"

She swatted my arm playfully. "You're too much. No, he'd lose his mind if he heard that his daughter was doing a "come have me" kind of a dance in a club, only to have been taken by his client."

We talked for a while till Sehgal returned. He looked expectantly between the two of us. "Well?"

I looked at Zeya, who was smiling secretly, and cleared my throat.

"Mr. Sehgal, Zeya's a lovely woman. If you allow me, I'd love to take her out to dinner this weekend."

Zeya's smile lit up the room.

***

It's been two years since then. After we began dating exclusively, Mr. Sehgal was the happiest. A year ago, he succumbed to his cancer and passed away. Zeya still mourns him. I can't blame her; they were exceptionally close.

Today, it's our anniversary. I take her to the same club where we had first met, which, thanks to Zeya, is now a classy place, and the rooftop of the building has turned into another fine dining. My heart sings with joy every time the patrons stare at the ambience with slacked jaws. I take Zeya up there blindfolded. She takes off the blindfold to a view of the rooftop decorated with vanilla orchids and yellow fairy lights, her favourite. The Way You Look Tonight plays softly in the background.

"Samar, this is –"

"Marry me."

"What?"

"Before I met you, I was a normal and happy guy going about his life. But now, I'm happier, jollier, everything a bit more than I used to be. I love being that way. I want to see your gorgeous eyes looking into no one else's but mine every morning. I want to be the one to make your morning coffee, your whiskey neat; I want to be the man for you. Will you marry me?"

"Yes," she smiles.

***

Six Months Later

Zeya

I gaze outside the window. Honeymooning in Switzerland is so mesmerising. Samar has gone down to the reception to arrange for a private lunch up in the mountains in a secluded cabin. It is funny how having money can get you things you wouldn't have otherwise even afforded.

I load my revolver and keep it stacked out of view. I check my ticket to Italy and make sure it's hidden well. Eight hours before I reunite with Bijoy. I smile at the thought of him.

I hear the front door of our suite open, and I hide the bag in my big suitcase.

"Love? I got us the cabin. I just need to pay half the amount in advance."

"That's great, sweetie."

He switches on his laptop. Fifteen minutes pass by, and I can see him struggling.

"That's weird," he murmurs and makes a call. "Yes, hi, this is Samar Ahuja. I'm having trouble accessing my savings account. Why does my account balance read nil? Yes, that would help. Thank you." He hangs up and looks at me. "They're looking into it."

In less than a minute, he gets a call again. "Hi. Yes. No, that can't be right. What are you talking about? I didn't transfer all the money to Sehgal and Associates. Mr. Sehgal was naturally the primary holder. He passed away two years ago, you dimwit. How could he have transferred the money to his company? If it was a joint account, the second holder could only have been –"

He pauses. My back is to him, but I can picture his expression.

"Zeya?"

"Yes, darling?"

I turn around to face him, revolver in hand.

"Daddy dearest was such a fool – like you. Two fools blinded by love. Love is such a twisted game," I smile, gently caressing the revolver in my palms.

He stares at me, shocked. "I –"

Three bullets shoot out and puncture his chest.

I open the dossier on Bijoy and take a last look – Bijoy Sharma, 28, owner of Miriam's Resorts, listed as one of the top ten billionaires of India. I chuckle and walk out of the room, excitement bubbling in my veins. The next pawn is waiting.

Acknowledgements

Coming this far and becoming who I am today would not have been possible without them. I'd like to offer my heartfelt gratitude:

To Mom, Dad, and Grandma, for always believing in me, loving me for who I am, challenging me to always be better, and helping me improve every step of the way.

To Saloni Amritkar, one of my steady rocks through thick and thin, for never leaving my side, having the patience to know me inside and out, being there for me even on the days when I didn't feel worthy, and slapping me back to sanity, sometimes literally, whenever I needed it. You're not just my homie; you're my home.

To Inkfeathers Publishing, for providing one of the best platforms writers could have ever wished for, and for providing an abode for writers to grow, evolve, connect, and embrace the best versions of themselves.

MEET THE
CO-AUTHORS

Susan Bowman

Susan Bowman discovered her talent as a writer quite late in life but successfully had several stories and poetry included in anthologies and publications to raise funds for NHS. She is working on her first novel and a poetry collection.

Prajwal Shukla

Prajwal Shukla is a prolific writing practitioner, enthusiast and has written over 440 short stories, blogs and articles on socio-economic issues and has a multitude of interests. He likes to explore conceptual fiction writing and a variety of topics in non-fiction as well. Here are the links to his profiles on Instagram, where he goes by @Storando and @prajwal_shukla

Yashika Rawal

Yashika Rawal is studying literature at Delhi University. Besides writing, you can find her reading novels. Being a bibliophile, she wishes to have her own library someday with shelves filled with hers' and her favourite authors' books.

Saloni Wagle

Being a talkative soul, words have always meant a lot to Saloni. But it wasn't until she put them down on paper, that she realised they weren't just her necessity, but her passion. She was immediately intoxicated by the feeling of gratification of completing a piece, and thus began her journey as a writer. Though she enjoys writing prose as well, her poems what she is most proud of.

Srikanth Palaparthy

Srikanth Palaparthy was born and raised in Hyderabad. He's an engineering graduate with a knack for writing dark and character-driven stories. He loves football and FIFA. Most Saturday nights you can find him, not at any pubs but in front of his TV cheering for FC Barcelona or Leeds United.

Hari Pudipeddi

Hari loves to create and tell stories; writes short fiction and poetry. He reads anything except romance. And is interested in studying philosophy and psychology as a lifelong endeavour.

Akhilesh Mahender

Akhilesh has grown up in Hyderabad city. Besides writing prescriptions, his veins bleed verses of fiction. Been an addict; smoking memories black and white. Yeah, an introvert forever. 24*(not out).

Anamika Kundu

A fun-loving person who also happens to be an English teacher, Anamika Kundu loves to read, travel, listen to music, run half marathons, and play various sports. She has been privileged to travel across the country with her father and husband being officers in the Indian Army.

Nurturing is her passion, be it her students or her garden. A warm and friendly person, she states she has friends in every corner of the world. A voracious reader, she loves stories to read or narrate. She is happy her students connect with her inside and outside the classroom. Her rich experience covers many educational boards from CBSE to ICSE and IGCSE to IB curriculum. Even as she rejoices turning silver, her enthusiasm to learn has not diminished, demonstrating that age is just a number. You can follow her blog: https://lifestrialsandsuccesses.wordpress.com

Darshini Parthiban

Darshini is a dreamer who has always found refuge in her imaginary worlds. Inspired by authors breathing magic into words and bringing worlds to life, she has tried her hand at being on the other side of the story. A medical student by day and an aspiring writer by night, she is conquering the world one story at a time.

Sameem Hassain

Sameem Hassain Mohammad hails from Kakinada, Andhra Pradesh and presently working in non-IT field. A lover of books, cinema, and music. He wants reading to be espoused by all as a solace from the frenetic pace of this life. You can contact him through Instagram @sameem_hassain

Himanshu Sukhala

A student at Delhi University, Himanshu Sukhala likes to try everything that catches his eye. He can often be seen with a book or playing video games. A fun, loving guy, Himanshu often gets in trouble in his pursuit of fun. He describes his writing as a way of penning down the thoughts and dreams that come randomly into his mind. Oh and he loves Pokémon and anime.

Salbaz Sayyed

Salbaz Sayyed is from the heart of Goa which is known as Ponda. He loves to write poems, quotes, and stories from mind to heart. He also likes to sing, draw, and participate in stand-up talks. If you want to talk with him, follow him on Instagram @sallu__65

Kristin Carmen

Kristin Carmen is a Paralegal out of
Florida, USA. She is an inspirational
writer and poet. Kristin has spent the last
decade reading and writing on a diverse
genre of topics.

Sudha Ramnath

From being part of a ladies drama troupe
specialising in male roles to writing plays,
from living on a remote island near
Madagascar to skydiving from 18,000
feet, Sudha Ramnath has quite the
penchant for crafting experiences. She's
done the regular too – worked in a bank,
married a man who she says is the sane
part of her life, taught math and chemistry and is a "mad but
loving mom" to two blessings she calls children. While others like
her drew up grocery lists and laundry schedules, Sudha made
plans to live the moments and stuck by it – she made the
pilgrimage to Alaska to see the Aurora Borealis, danced like there
was no tomorrow at a flash mob in San Francisco and stood by
the Ngorongoro crater in Tanzania. This collection of thrillers is
then another off the bucket-list and a dream come true but true to
her spirit, there's bound to more for where there is an end, Sudha
sees a beginning.

Karthik C

Karthik C is a Bangalore-based writer of speculative fiction. His publishing credits include short stories, awareness articles, award-winning blogs, and a thriller novel. He has a Master's in Microbiology and works as a Project Manager for a research organization.

Deepshikha Saw

Deepshikha Saw is a professional tennis player. She has won many titles and medals. She is pursuing graduation in Economics from Gujarat University, India. She has participated in various writing competitions and workshops. Her writing has been acclaimed by mass readers. You can connect with her on Instagram @deeps.shivangi7.

Santhosh Ganesan

Santhosh Ganesan is a writer, 3D Visual Artist and screenwriter from Kumbakonam, Tamil Nadu. His interest and passion for filmmaking is deep-rooted. You can connect with him and find his work on Instagram by the handle @santhoshpotter

Manish Nair

Manish M Nair Manish is a Quality Engineer by profession and an artist by passion. He also writes poetry and his story Vengeance - is published in the anthology 'Three Bodies One Soul'. For him, writing is to re-create the reality. You can connect with him on Instagram @nair_manish_

Manoj Vaz

Manoj has published five books: Tinsel - a hard look at Mumbai's Show Biz, The Kidnapping and Meth Mystery — both for teenagers, Kaleidoscope – his personal collection of short stories and poems and Random Musings - a collection of his quotes.

Geetika K. Bakshi

Geetika K. Bakshi works in an African consulate and is a French-language trainer. Writing is her passion. She has published a book as well, with the name of Ibiza by Geetika Kaura and is now a published co-author. She is always glad to meet people with the same passion. Her Instagram profile is @geetikakbakshi

Aaron Dsouza

Aaron is a budding author who dabbles in poetry and prose while attempting to recreate the world with a dramatic flair through his writing.

D. H. Holmes

Hailing from the rolling green hills of West Yorkshire, England, D.H. left for Australia in 2015, with thirty-odd countries already under his belt. Bound to the written word, you'll find him in a Sydney café, with his nose in a book, and coffee in his moustache. His writings range from slipstream fiction to poetry; and a debut novel underway. Join him on Instagram @about.which.

INKFEATHERS PUBLISHING

India's Most Author Friendly Publishing House

Stay updated about latest books, anthologies, events, exclusive offers, contests, product giveaways and other things that we do to support authors.

 Inkfeathers Publishing

 @InkfeathersPublishing

 @_Inkfeathers

 @Inkfeathers

 Inkfeathers.com

We'd love to connect with you!

9 788195 020577